MY NAME IS
SUNSHINE
SIMPSON

G.M. LINTON

Illustrated by Fuuji Takashi and Emily Bornoff

USBORNE

Auntie Sharon

Dariuszkz

Granny Cynthie &
Grampie Clive

Mum & Dad

Meet my family – and welcome to my rollercoaster life!

Me (age 6)

Grandad Bobby

The Twinzies (Lena & Peter)

"Only when it is dark enough can you see

the stars."

Dr Martin Luther King Jr

Hello.

My name is Sunshine Simpson and I'm very pleased to meet you.

I don't entirely know why I'm starting the story this way, it just seems like a proper introduction. Polite.

Actually, I do know why I'm starting the story this way. I want to ask you a question and I didn't want to launch into it by throwing myself at you too quickly. That seemed rude.

But now I've got the good manners part done, here goes...

Have you ever wished you had a **magic button** that you could press to play back all the best bits of everything that happens to you, but then delete all the bad bits that you don't like as much? I have, but no magic button has ever appeared. If it had, maybe my life would be different now.

I must warn you: there are no wizards or any **magic** fixes in this story to make everything better — although there are a few unicorns and a dragon (sort of). And there are things you'll find out that have changed my world for ever. I know that sounds a bit dramatic, but it's true — I've been through **big-time drama** of the highest order lately.

I should let you judge for yourselves really, so I'm going to get on with telling you what actually happened. It's always best to start a story at the beginning. Well, that's what my teacher, Miss Peach, tells me. She says a good story always has a beginning, a middle and an end. Miss Peach is very wise, despite being named after a fruit, so I'll follow her advice, and take you back to the beginning of last summer term, when everything started to go horribly wrong.

1

HORSEY OLD LADY FACE

Focus. Power, I chanted under my breath. **Focus. Power. You've got this, Sunshine. You've. Got. This.**

Near the start of every summer term, each class at my school takes part in a skipping fitness challenge. All the kids gather in their classes on the school playground and playing fields, kind of like a mini sports day, and have to do as many skips as possible in one minute, using posh skipping ropes with in-built counters. The top skippers from each class get to have their photo and name displayed on the **Wall of Fame** in the school hall.

The Wall of Fame is really called **"the celebration wall"**, and you get to be on it whenever you do anything great at school, but us kids have always called it the Wall of Fame to pep things up a bit. Give it a bit of **star quality**. Being good at skipping was my claim to fame. Maybe it was a small claim to fame, but it meant a lot to me.

Even though the teachers always said, "It's not a competition, it's the taking part that counts", I'd won the "it's not a competition" skipping challenge for two years in a row — so this time I was going for the hat-trick of three wins. But this time, as it turned out, was different.

You see, I have a friend called Evie Evans. She started at our school at the beginning of the school year, last September. And Evie is brilliant — at *everything*.

Evie was skipping next to me and my heart heaved in my chest as I desperately tried to keep in time with her. I could feel my pride and my title literally skipping away from me.

Pocus. Fower, I told myself again. Huh? My focus was un-powering or my power was un-focusing. Whichever one it was, this wasn't a good sign.

I kept stealing glances at Evie. Watching her as she

jumped effortlessly, leaping like a gazelle, with her ponytail of dark, bouncing curls bobbing beautifully behind her; not even the tiniest bead of sweat on her forehead. My forehead looked like someone could dive in and take a swim in it.

When the minute was up, I'd got dead-on one hundred skips — five skips down on last year. But Evie had got 106 skips — the most in the whole class (the most **EVER**). I was the washed-up runner-up. Evie had won.

"Don't worry, Sunshine, you mustn't be down in the mouth about this," said Miss Peach, as she took a photo of a beaming Evie for the Wall of Fame. "It's not a competition, it's the taking part that counts."

Right.

"It's those long legs, Sunny. You're very gangly, aren't you." Evie told me (she wasn't asking). "**You need to focus.** Keep it all together so that you're not flopping about all over the place. Keep your back straight like I do.

DON'T raise your legs too high. And **DON'T** look down at your feet." Evie was giving me lessons, like she was the teacher and I was her pupil. If only she knew how hard I *had* been trying to focus. There was virtually smoke coming out of my ears.

My best friends, Charley and Arun, rolled their eyes, obviously very offended on my behalf. Charley and Arun always have my back. It's a shame they couldn't have held the skipping rope to help me go a bit faster too.

"I'm just not great at skipping any more, I guess," I said, realizing that I was now holding on to a bucketload of hurt as well as the useless skipping rope.

I mopped at my brow and then held my hand out to shake Evie's hand, fair and square. Evie made a squirmy face as she saw my sweaty palm approaching. And then, right on cue, accidentally proving the point that I wasn't great at skipping any more, I tangled my legs in the rope, tumbling to the ground like a chopped-down tree.

Evie's face lit up. "But you're really good at being silly! I love that about you," she laughed. "And your face goes all **crinkly like an old lady's** when you're concentrating on something. You almost put me off my skips! I'll have to start calling you **Silly Sunny**."

"Oh," I said, and then laughed a ridiculous, exaggerated laugh back at her.

I wasn't sure if I was meant to be offended or not. Crinkly old lady? I go to primary school!

And, yes, even though I am taller than a lot of other kids at Beeches Primary, and maybe because of that seem a bit older, I was sure I didn't need to buy a trolley load of wrinkle cream just yet. Or maybe I did?

I decided to check in with my Grandad Bobby after school. I could talk to my grandad about anything, even about looking like my own grandmother!

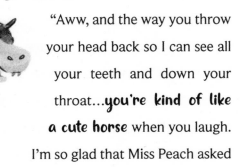

"Aww, and the way you throw your head back so I can see all your teeth and down your throat...**you're kind of like a cute horse** when you laugh. I'm so glad that Miss Peach asked

13

you to be my school buddy," said Evie.

I immediately shut my mouth. **A cute horse? Hmph!** Next she'd lead me to the playing fields and start feeding me a bag of apples and a few carrots.

But instead of saying anything, I raised my hand to wave Evie off as she happily skipped over to Miss Peach (this time without a skipping rope). I assumed they were both about to skip off together into the school hall and remove me from the Wall of Fame.

"You would have beaten Evie if you didn't keep looking across at her," said Arun, helping to free me from my ropey prison, and lifting me to my feet.

"Yes," said Charley. "You're a great skipper. You're good at lots of things, especially school stuff and gymnastics. Don't let her put you off."

I know you have to accept defeat as graciously as victory or whatever, but I'd been proud of being on the Wall of Fame. I'd never been the true champion of anything before. And, yes, Charley was right, I like school stuff — English and geography, even maths. But I had never been special, never particularly interesting. Even my gymnastics skills were basic. I could do the splits, one-handed cartwheel and a backwards walkover — which Charley seemed to think made me an Olympic champion like Simone Biles — but that was it. And now it was just a matter of time before I'd be erased from the Wall of Fame, replaced by Evie's angelic, smiling face.

I stamped my foot, not meaning to seem bad-tempered; it was more to remove the remaining rope, which had now seemingly come to life and was snaking its way back up my leg. "I don't let her put me off. I just need to raise my game," I said.

My friends shrugged. And that was what I was going to do — shrug the whole **horsey, crinkly-old-lady-face** thing off and start all over again. Or so I thought.

2

ALL ABOUT EVIE

I was Evie's official **"school buddy"**.

She was new in town, so I'd been assigned to look after her when she started at school. I was meant to show her the ropes — but definitely not skipping ropes! It was more like where the toilets were, having lunch with her, teaming-up on school projects, that sort of thing. **So life became all about Evie.**

In the early days it was a dream. I really enjoyed hanging out with Evie and learned quite a lot about her. Like how her proper first name is Evonne, because she was named after one of her grandmothers.

Evie told me she didn't like her proper name because it was "**soooo old-fashioned**", and that, secretly, she immediately hated anyone (except her parents) who used it — even teachers! She said I was the only person she'd ever told about the secret hating thing. I mean, I actually thought it wasn't everyone else's fault that she was called Evonne and at least it was different, but I didn't say that. Instead I'd beamed, full of a secret I would never tell. I got the feeling that Evie had lots of secrets that she never told anyone about. But I was prepared to give her time to settle in, to win her trust, because I liked Evie and I thought Evie liked me.

Evie's favourite drink in the whole, wide world was **hot chocolate with gooey marshmallows, cream and chocolate sprinkles on top, just like mine**! And we loved the same **music**. Evie would tell me what songs she liked to listen to on her phone. Yes, Evie had **her own phone**! I've always wanted my own phone, but could never persuade my parents to get me one. Evie had the

best phone money could buy, by the look of it. It looked more expensive than a *house*! I wasn't envious I told myself, just appreciative.

Evie was great.

I'd overheard Evie's dad tell my grandad that their family moved up to where we live from somewhere called the Home Counties, because Evie's mum was "from this part of the world and she wanted to come home". They'd both managed to transfer their jobs, which had made the move easier. Evie's mum does important things with computers and her dad is a lawyer. And they both used to commute into the **"big city"** for work.

"Ooh, posh," said Mum when Grandad told her.

"Oh," I said. I'd never heard of the Home Counties before. And I didn't know what commuting into the big city meant. But it gave Evie — and her family — that additional air of mystery. I was loving it.

I like to learn about places, especially places I've never been to before, so I jotted it all down in my little notebook, where I write down ***Things and places of interest*** to look up later.

Our house is pretty busy —
I live with my mum, dad and my
twin brother and sister, and my
mum's dad, my Grandad Bobby,
also lived with us. But Evie only
lives with her mum and dad

since her older sister, Hannah-Jade, went to university in
London and only visits in the holidays.

Even though Evie and her family had moved to be
closer to her mum's relatives, I thought about how Evie
was probably lonely without her old school friends and her
sister, and what with leaving all she knew behind to come
and live in the West Midlands. And I didn't want her to feel
alone.

As it turned out, Evie may have been far away from the
Home Counties, but she certainly made herself quite at
home at Beeches Primary. She quickly turned into the **star
student** in our class.

If you could make a model of a perfect student, they
would probably look and act like Evie. She's really clever
and everything about her is neat and tidy: perfectly ironed

school uniform; two rows of perfectly straight, sparkling teeth; perfectly pouting mouth. Even the cool dark freckles on her warm brown face look like they've been neatly laid out on either side of her nose in a precise and perfect order. She has big brown eyes like **luminous full moons** beneath a lush forest of perfectly fluttering eyelashes. And her dark brown curls seem to bounce perfectly in time with her footsteps as she moves. She always ties her hair neatly away in a ponytail and wears a hairband to stop her curls falling into her eyes. But if I was her, I'd let my curls fly free. They're perfect too.

I know I'm using the word perfect quite a lot here, and I should be using a wider-ranging vocabulary, as Miss Peach would no doubt tell me. But it's true: Evie is practically perfect in every way.

I'm tall and lanky. I'm never quite sure what to do with myself, as my arms and legs keep getting in the way. It's like I've been stretched as far as I can go and never shrunk back again. Elastic-band girl. I get it from my dad. His height would make a **giraffe** bow its neck in adoration.

Evie holds her head high with such confidence. I wished I could do that. Even though my mum always said I should **"stand tall and proud"**, I'd often stoop to make myself look a little shorter, just to feel like I was fitting in with everyone else.

And it was easy to sink into the background once Evie joined our school. That became clearer as the days went by.

3
AND THIS IS WHY X IS IMPORTANT TO ME

After the skipping challenge, Miss Peach made an announcement in class that afternoon.

"I have exciting news!" she said, clapping her hands together in delight. We all sat up straight in our chairs. "You will be aware, class, that this year we are celebrating the Golden Jubilee of Beeches School. Fifty years! Isn't that amazing? And the Spring Bazaar we held last month in celebration was a real triumph. We raised so many funds to maintain our lovely school."

Ancient history. We all slumped in our seats.

"I have more news," chimed Miss Peach, realizing she

was losing her audience. We un-slumped ourselves. "Mrs Honeyghan, our beloved head teacher, wants every class to take part in further celebrations."

YEESS! We all looked around at each other excitedly, imagining a **massive party with cake... sweets...ice cream...music...dancing! PARRTAAYY! HAPPY BIRTHDAY, BEECHES SCHOOL!**

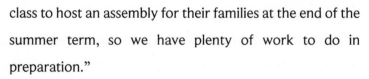

"Just to be *clear*," said Miss Peach, coughing slightly, "Mrs Honeyghan wants each and every class to host an assembly for their families at the end of the summer term, so we have plenty of work to do in preparation."

Well, that sounded about as exciting as a slowly deflating balloon.

Miss Peach did her best to try and reinflate the balloon. "Mrs Honeyghan would like each class to theme their assemblies. This got me thinking. What is a school without its students?"

Miss Peach looked out at a sea of blank faces.

"Empty. A school is an empty shell without its pupils," she said. "You, and all the children who have come before you, make this school special. You make it come alive! I want everyone — teachers, pupils, your families — to discover more about you. Your inspirations, your hopes, your dreams, and why they are important to **you**. So, I am setting our assembly topic as ***And this is why X is important to me***. X could be a hobby or talent you could demonstrate, such as singing or dancing, or maybe X is someone who inspires you in the local community who you could share a story about. We do not need **bells and whistles**, but we do need your **hearts**."

Miss Peach was beside herself with glee. I was beside myself with terror. This sounded like an absolutely awful project. I wasn't too keen on the idea of standing in front of anyone and giving bells, whistles or my heart, because:

1. **I wouldn't have anything interesting to say; and**
2. **Something usually goes disastrously wrong whenever I do anything in front of an audience** (you'll see what I mean). Except for the skipping, I suppose, but even that had now taken a nosedive.

24

"Mrs Honeyghan says the idea 'really demonstrates the spirit of the school'," said Miss Peach proudly.

I was all for "**the spirit of the school**", but felt it would have been far more convenient to display our spirit in some other way, like sitting quietly in a corner or meditating underneath a tree.

But then again, I thought, maybe this was my chance to make a big comeback after my epic skipping fail. If I could think of something brilliant to do at the Golden Jubilee assembly, then maybe — just maybe — I could be the star of the show and make it back onto the Wall of Fame!

"Does anyone want to share something with the class that might provide some inspiration for the assembly? Maybe about a person, or perhaps a trip or a special memory?" trilled Miss Peach.

"**I will,**" Evie piped up without a moment's hesitation. She didn't even raise her hand, **LIKE WE'RE SUPPOSED TO, she just launched herself like a rocket**. "I have so many ideas spinning around in my head, but can I share about my family's last summer holiday?"

"Yes, go ahead." Miss Peach clapped with increasing delight.

I had to hold back my sigh, but it swelled within me. These days, everything was about Evie. But I had to hand it to her, the girl knew how to tell a seriously good story.

Apparently, Evie and her parents had travelled to somewhere called Lake Como in Italy for a **"dream holiday"**, because her mum had always wanted to go there. She said it was **"enchanting and magical"**, with its shimmering waters, mountainous views, pretty gardens and beautiful buildings. They got to zip around in a **speedboat**. And there were lots of rich and famous people who swanned around in glamorous clothes, dripping in **jewellery**. They even met some actor called George Clooney, Evie told us.

"Did you really?" asked Miss Peach, who was totally

engrossed and turning what I can only call salmon-pink from the thrill of it all.

"Well," said Evie, a little sheepishly, and adjusting her hairband so that her curls didn't fall down into her eyes, "we didn't meet him exactly, but we saw the back of his head as he drove past us in a posh sports car with his wife."

I mean, that could have been anyone, but why ruin a good story? It wasn't so much what Evie was saying, but the way she said it in that sing-songy excitable voice of hers that had us all hanging on to her every word like pigeons feasting on tossed crumbs in a park.

If I'd been telling the story my voice definitely wouldn't have had the same effect, as it's a bit gravelly and croaky — Evie once told me it sounds like I have a permanent bad cold. Plus the furthest place I've ever been is Devon and, as far as I know, **George Dooley** has never visited there. We did see a Sooty-and-Sweep-type puppet show one day when we were at the beach — and when I was chosen to go up to the front **to shake the puppets' paws, I accidentally pulled one of them off the puppeteer's hand** and some of the adults laughed and some of the children cried, but that's another story.

Anyway, Evie sparkled with her Italian **I've-met-a-famous-actor-and-you-haven't-so-there** tale. She twirled a curl from her ponytail around one of her fingers, slanting her head slightly to one side as she spoke. Part of me hoped she'd get a cricked neck.

But as she walked back to her desk, she flashed me the most brilliant smile. I took in such a sharp breath at how dazzling it was that I immediately paid for my mean thoughts and started choking in my seat.

"Are you okay, Sunshine?" Miss Peach called.

If Miss Peach had been salmon-pink a moment ago, she now turned ghostly white, and I was turning beetroot-purple. She came over and started patting me vigorously on the back. "Go fetch Sunshine's water bottle from the tray!" she shouted to anyone within earshot.

At one point I thought she was going to hoick me out of my seat and start doing that **High Mick manoeuvre** thingy, like I've seen people on TV do to save someone's life. Little did she know that I was only choking on my own venom.

Evie came over to my desk when I'd stopped coughing and we had settled down for lessons. "Are you okay?"

she asked. "You had me worried for a minute."

I touched my throat. "I'm fine now, thanks. Some air just went down the wrong way."

"Well, that's good." She smiled. "Silly Sunny. I was worried everyone would think you were just trying to be the centre of attention."

If Evie knew anything about me, she'd know that wasn't true. Any time I am the centre of attention, I end up doing something...well...embarrassing. Like the time I tripped over my smock when I walked onto the stage to narrate the school nativity and sent the **donkey* flying** into the front row of the audience. Or the time my dress got stuck in my pants when I was bridesmaid at my godmother Patsy's wedding, and no one noticed until we all got up to join the bride and groom for their first dance.

I do not like being centre stage. And that reminded me that I would probably be a disaster at our Golden Jubilee class assembly.

I stayed quiet for the rest of the afternoon.

*A real donkey wasn't hurt in the nativity incident. It was Marcus Cruickshank, dressed in grey and wearing bunny-rabbit ears. His mum said it was a shame to waste the ears left over from Easter.

4

TAXI!

I glumly flapped the trowel about as I "helped" Grandad **sow flower seeds** around the borders in our back garden after school. Grandad wanted us to get on top of little jobs so that the garden would be "**in glorious bloom**" during the summer.

Neither rain, sun, wind nor snow could stop Grandad tending his garden. He was ready for every season.

Me and my six-year-old brother and sister, Peter and Lena — or **the Twinzies** as I call them, for no other reason than they are twins and it's quicker to shout **"TWINZIES!"** when I want to speak to them both at the same time — took it in turns to help Grandad quite a bit these days.

We have a lovely garden, with decking, a lawn and borders, a little greenhouse and a "man cave" shed, which Grandad and my dad shared so they could do all kinds of pottering about. But
Grandad had been feeling too achy to manage the garden by himself since he'd caught a cold over Easter. He'd started to tire very quickly, which wasn't like him at all. He was "**creakier than an old floorboard and sleepier than a bear in winter**". Those were Grandad's words, not mine.

Grandad used to be a bodybuilder when he was younger and won loads of competitions. His nickname was **Iron Bobby**. He'd made the mistake of telling our neighbour, Mrs Turner, about his competitions once, and since then **she'd treated him like one of the Avengers**. She had him climbing trees, going up ladders, down ditches and all sorts, fixing things for her.

Grandad was shaped like an ox, had hands the size of Christmas hams, and fingers like juicy sausages. He was strong enough to do anything, in our minds. But **the Twinzies** and me were happy to help him for a change, because Grandad was always helping us. He dropped us off and picked us up from school every day, and then looked after us until our parents got home from work. Grandad was always on the go. We knew he'd recover from his cold soon. Nothing could keep Grandad down for long.

Usually we'd be chitter-chattering about school as we worked, but I didn't feel like saying much on that day. I didn't even bother telling Grandad about losing my **skipping crown**.

Besides, I had the Golden Jubilee assembly to think about now. **What was I going to do?** And how was I going to make sure I didn't make a fool of myself doing it? These were the two main questions rolling around inside my head. As for Evie, whatever she ended up doing would have the whole audience lapping it up like cats at a bowl of water, I was one hundred per cent sure of that.

"Grandad, every class has to put on an assembly for their families to celebrate the school's Golden Jubilee. Do you think I could do something with a gardening theme?

Also, do you think I need to use wrinkle cream?" I asked, skilfully and delicately slipping in the skincare question.

Grandad stopped tending to the **climbing rose**, his favourite plant in the garden, and looked towards the bright blue sky in thought. "Hmm…now that is an idea. **Bringing the outside indoors, mi like it!** And…it's always helpful to moisturize…yes. But I don't think you need to worry about wrinkles for a good few decades yet."

I smiled. Grandad had a way of cutting through nonsense without even directly talking about it.

"So, what are you thinking? About the assembly, mi mean, not the cream," asked Grandad, smiling back at me.

Oh! I hadn't thought that far ahead. I had no plan. Not yet.

I couldn't exactly dig up Grandad's prized climbing rose, stick it in the middle of the stage in the school hall and give the audience a pruning demonstration. Though it would have been nice to use it. Grandad called the rose **Pepper**, after his wife, my long-lost Grandma Pepper. Whenever I look at it, it kind of makes me feel closer to her. And I think it did the same thing for Grandad too.

Grandma Pepper and Grandad Bobby had taken my mum and her sister — my Auntie Sharon — to live in Jamaica when they were children, years ago. But Mum and Auntie Sharon "couldn't settle", so Grandad and Grandma Pepper brought them back to live in England. But then Grandma Pepper "couldn't settle" back here either, so she returned to **Jamaica**, because that's where she was born and still had family. Grandad stayed here with Mum and Auntie Sharon. In the beginning, Grandad used to travel backwards and forwards to see Grandma, and I think there were plans for him to return to live there with her, but then after my Auntie Sharon had her son, and when I and then **the Twinzies** were born, Grandad decided to stay here permanently with us.

Grandma Pepper doesn't come back to England much. She came to visit when we were each born, but always went back home to Jamaica. She says it's too cold for her bones and her throat. My Grandma Pepper is a singer.

And then Grandma Pepper did the thing that I would

love to do one day: she left Jamaica and went travelling — all around the world, singing on cruise ships — and she eventually settled in America.

But still, when the mood took her, she would set off on her travels again, far and wide.

No one could keep up with her, not even Grandad. He stopped travelling to see her as often after a while. And then I guess he must have stopped completely, but I don't remember when.

Imagine all the countries my grandma has seen! Amazing! And sometimes Grandma Pepper would send us candy and other treats from abroad. **Yum!**

Mum is less impressed with Grandma. "She's prickly and beautiful and showy, just like that rose of yours that you gaze at all the time," I overheard her say to Grandad once, in a huff.

"Maybe so. Maybe so. But try not to be too harsh. Your mother was born to roam," said Grandad. "Some people just need to be free." And then Mum double-huffed and stalked off.

No one talks about "**the situation with Grandma Pepper**" any more really. So I just keep my trap shut. Mostly.

"Who am I kidding, Grandad? A gardening demonstration would never work. How could I make that interesting?" I said, getting cross with myself.

"Chuh, man! Nonsense!" scolded Grandad. "Gardening is a great idea. And, besides, you're more interesting than most. Do you remember what happened the day you were born?"

Well, obviously, technically, I don't remember anything at all from that day, because I was only just squawking my way into the world, but the story usually gets wheeled out at Christmas, birthdays and any other special occasion where Grandad can weave it into the conversation.

Apart from being skipping champion, it's the only interesting thing that's ever happened to me in the history of my life, so it's a shame I can't remember it for myself. I've always lived the excitement through Grandad.

"Yes, Grandad. But that was then and this is now. Right now, I'm about as interesting as a...as a tomato sandwich!"

Clearly, this wasn't the best example to give a man who devoted so much time to looking **after his fruit and vegetables**. But tomatoes were the first thing that popped into my head, because Grandad always insisted on growing them and Mum made us eat them. Grandad immediately broke into a rap on the spot.

"Tomatoes, tomatoes,
They make your heart go.
If I were a tomato,
I'd be so smart though.

"You hear that, Sunshine? I'm up with the kids, hey!"

"It's *down* with the kids, Grandad," I giggled.

"Up, down, all around. Who cares? **Make your own lyrics in life**. It makes the adventure more fun. And I'll let you into a secret. Tomatoes are one of the best fruits in the world – even though most people think they're vegetables! They're one of the most exciting things out there – animal, vegetable, mineral and — **T.O.M.A.T.O.E.S**. — tomatoes!"

I was really giggling now and trying to get into the spirit of things. "I guess so. And there are plenty to choose from. You always do say that about tomatoes."

"Yes, very true. But you must remember, there's only one you," said Grandad.

I shrugged, suddenly losing hope again. "I suppose so."

"You suppose so! How many people share the same story as you, **girly-whirly**?"

I didn't reply.

"Chuh, man! Very few, my sweet Sunshine, very few."

Grandad Bobby would always say I am destined to shine because of the way I came into the world. I know every part of the story about how I was born word-for-word as I've heard it so many times.

Basically, Grandad and Mum had just got back from the supermarket. They were in Grandad's car because Mum's car was at the mechanic's getting fixed.

Mum absolutely would not take the easy option and use the laptop, do a few clicks, and have a fridge full of delicious food delivered straight to her doorstep. Oh no, that would be too easy. You see, Mum refuses to do any shopping on the internet — she loathes it. The internet is not her friend, "**It's my best enemy**", that's what she says.

"**I like to know what's going into my trolley, thank you.**"

"**I don't need anyone else choosing for me, thank you.**"

"**I don't want goods with tomorrow's use-by date, thank you.**"

Mum will say the same thing at least three times in different ways, just so she knows you're listening — and she always says "**thank you**" at the end, so no one thinks she's being rude.

I think Mum's a bit afraid of the modern world. It's as if she expects the computer mouse to jump up and bite her on the nose or something.

Anyway, Grandad tried to wrestle Mum into the house before she had a chance to get the shopping bags out of the boot of the car.

"You have sense, Cheryl? You pregnant or you have a football up your jumper? Mi can manage. You go and sit down and rest yourself," said Grandad, tugging a bag away from Mum's hand.

Mum was in the middle of saying, "I may be the size of a two-bedroom bungalow, but I can still move," when she started feeling funny and getting pains in her belly, and then, all of a sudden, she really couldn't move because the pains were coming so fast.

"Come, mi will drive you to the hospital," said Grandad.

"I'm not going in that old contraption again. Not if you pay me! It sounds like it's going to break down any minute by the racket that engine's making!"

"Chuh! Is where mi get you from? Get in the car. You want to have the baby on the street?"

Then Mum must have **"seen sense"** because she managed to bundle herself into the car, Grandad grabbed her maternity bag from the house, and they made their way to the hospital.

Halfway there, **the car started to stutter, burp and jump**, and Mum heard Grandad muttering some rude words under his breath. Then the car just stopped dead, like a metal statue on four wheels, right in the middle of the road.

"What's happening?" Mum spluttered through her panting.

"Just breathe, Cheryl. Keep breathing," said Grandad through gritted teeth.

Mum started shouting through the panting. "Of course I'm breathing. I'm over-breathing! What's wrong with this old rust bucket?"

"You see how you put your mouth on the car?" said Grandad, remembering to be hurt, even in the middle of all the panic, that Mum had just insulted his beloved "rust bucket". "Is where your phone?"

But Mum had forgotten her **phone** at home when they'd gone shopping.

"What's the point of calling it a mobile if you forget to carry it anywhere?" said Grandad, making a very sensible point. "There's nothing else to do then."

Like a superhero coming to the rescue, he jumped out of the car waving his arms, half like he was directing traffic and half like he was trying to take off into the sky.

The next thing Mum knew, she was being bundled out of the car and into a taxi that Grandad had flagged down as it passed by.

The taxi driver drove so fast in the panic — "**like Lewis Hamilton after drinking too much fizzy pop,**" Grandad always said — that the sound of sirens could suddenly be heard behind them. By the time the taxi driver pulled over and two police officers loomed over the car, my head was coming out.

"'Ello, 'ello, 'ello," said the officers. (They didn't really say that, Grandad always added that bit for dramatic effect — and Mum always double-rolled her eyes.)

But, anyway, one of the officers had to deliver me because it was too late to get to the hospital. And there you have it: **I was born in the back of a taxi under police guard.**

"It's a shame it wasn't a black cab," Mum always says and sighs as she looks at the photo on the mantelpiece. It's of all of us in the newspaper: a beaming Grandad, ecstatic Dad, a tired-looking Mum, two smiling police officers, a shocked-looking taxi driver, with his gleaming silver car in the background as a special guest of honour, and a big-headed baby (**me!**).

And that's where I come to why my name is my name.

"Look how she burst into the world, there's no stopping her. And see how her face is so big and bright? You should call her Sunshine," Grandad said a few days later, once Mum had recovered from the shock of it all.

"NO! Daddy, people will laugh," said Mum.

"**Chuh!** You too English! You care too much 'bout what other people think," said Grandad.

It was Dad who found a way, like he always does, to keep both Mum and Grandad happy. Everyone calls me Sunshine, but the name that's on my birth certificate is Karis Sunshine Simpson.

"We can call her Sunshine as her pet name," said Dad. **"Let's do it Jamaican *stylee*."**

Then Grandad smiled. Mum smiled. They all smiled. And so everyone who knew Grandad — which is basically everyone in this town — calls me Sunshine. Hardly anyone, except for Mum, uses Karis. I suppose it's a little bit like Evonne being Evie.

All I can say is, it's a good job they didn't call me Bazza after the taxi driver.

I bet Evie wasn't born in the back of a taxi. Knowing her, she was probably born in a **chariot** or a posh sports car or something — and delivered by the actor George Boomey, no doubt.

"Hold your head up, sweet Sunshine," Grandad said, bringing me back to the garden and my assembly dilemma. "**Let no one — let no-thing — steal your joy.** You're a bright light in this universe, our very own **Sunshine.** Now let's get back to work. Keep sowing for your old grandad, while I look after **Rose Pepper.** You have to give plants love and attention to help them grow." Grandad smiled.

"Maybe I could grow a plant or some vegetables and bring them in to talk about for the assembly, Grandad?"

"That's my girl."

I nodded and smiled. Grandad had cheered me up. Grandad always had that special way of making me feel better. But I still wasn't convinced about the gardening. Grandad standing up on the stage would make any fruit or vegetable — even a **tomato** — sound interesting, but I wasn't so sure I'd inherited the same talent.

I had some serious work to do to make myself seem interesting. But I didn't realize that seeming interesting would be such a tough job.

5

DUCK!

At dinner that evening I set about doing some hard thinking, which basically meant me furrowing my eyebrows a lot, squinting my eyes, and ending up giving myself a headache.

Oof! Every year, school seems to get harder. I don't know about **With great power comes great responsibility**, like Spider-Man's uncle says — it's more like, with an extra year added at every birthday comes more work to do. That's my reality. I wonder if trees get stressed out the more rings they get?

Mum was busy cooking. Her and Dad took it in turns to make dinner, like a tag team.

Mum didn't like Grandad making the main meal — she said he did enough for us all already. But secretly I think she reckoned that if she left Grandad to his own devices, he would just feed us on biscuits and cakes all the time, until sugar came out of our ears. She must have a sixth sense, because Grandad would regularly give us "**just a little something**" before Mum or Dad got back. This could be treats like Jamaican mint balls, or tangy, sticky and sweet tamarind balls, that would make our mouths sing with a zing.

"If Mum ever finds out, **our gooses, never mind the treats, will be well and truly cooked**," Grandad would say with a laugh. So we all kept it a sweet secret. Just between me, Grandad and **the Twinzies**.

I could have tried to tap Mum up for topics for the assembly while she was rushing around finishing off the meal, but Mum is a bit rubbish with anything creative — that's why she has a plain and sensible job, I suppose. In fact, thinking about it, both Mum and Dad do very boring things for a living.

Dad is an accountant, which means he looks after money for people with money. **"I make sure the numbers**

add up," is what Dad says all pretend-menacingly and in a funny accent, like he's some kind of gangster mafia accountant (he is not). He watches too many movies.

Mum is a debt adviser, so she looks after people who don't have any money at all and shows them how to get themselves **"back on track"**, which I suppose is even more sensible and boring than Dad's job. She doesn't have the pizazz of Grandma Pepper or Grandad Bobby.

"Where's Grandad?" I asked.

"Oh, he's just feeling a little tired after being in the garden, so he's having a lie-down," said Mum.

"A lie-down? Again?" I asked.

"Yes, a nap," said Mum.

I couldn't understand why Mum didn't find this recent turn of events as strange or as troubling as I did. Grandad Bobby never used to take naps in the daytime like you would expect old people to — but he had started to do it quite a lot lately. This was the ox-man. And even at eighty-two years old, he could still walk faster than most and beat people years younger than him when challenged to an arm-wrestling competition. A couple of years before, he'd **stopped a robbery** at Suresh Chanda's grocery store. Grandad Bobby had crept up on the robber from behind and **bopped him really hard on the head with a multi-pack of tinned tuna,** followed quickly by a massive bag of rice, and then Grandad Bobby sat on the robber and ate a bag of bonbons, all casually, until the police came.

The police said they "wouldn't recommend that course of action to foil a robbery of any kind" but that Grandad was "very brave", and they gave him an **Outstanding Citizen Award** for his heroics.

So what I'm trying to say is, **my grandad did NOT take daytime naps.** A bit of gardening was as easy as lifting a feather for Grandad, usually — but maybe his cold was getting him down more than I'd first thought. Things do when they drag on for a bit, don't they?

There was no point in asking Mum any more about

it though. Not while she was cooking (Mum takes her cooking very seriously), and especially with the extra dimension of **the Twinzies** yapping in her ear.

"What's for dinner, Mum?" shouted Lena Twinzie.

"Duck and pancakes," said Mum.

As she'd paused to answer Lena's question, I seized the opportunity to ask Mum about the jubilee assembly. I cleared my throat and threw my best Mum-like death stare at Lena to try and shut her up. "Did you know, we have to '**think outside the box**' and do something creative for our class's assembly to celebrate the school's fifty-year jubilee?" I began.

"Mr Bishop's going to write our class a **song** — and then we'll get to dress up in costumes and sing it," interrupted Peter Twinzie.

A monster with green eyes appeared at my shoulder. **The Twinzies'** class assembly sounded like it was going to be fun and super easy! Why couldn't Mr Bishop write a song for me?

This time it was Peter's turn for my greatest death stare. "If I may continue," I said snottily, "*my* class's assembly is based on the theme **And this is why X is important to me**."

"We don't know anybody called X," said Lena Twinzie.

I rolled my eyes. "Yes, we do, **Malcolm X**."

"Malcolm X — that's a funny name. Who's he?"

I ignored her, even though I knew the answer. Malcolm X was a leader in something called the civil rights movement which helped to fight racism in America. It's amazing how what my parents say can occasionally stick like glue, even when I'm not listening properly.

"Why don't you talk about the family or draw a picture of something you love and talk about that?" suggested Mum.

I could barely hide my disgust. "That is *too* predictable, Mum. I am not six years old! I will be eleven soon." Mum flashed me a look. "Well, soon-ish," I continued. "And I am not going to stand up in our class's jubilee celebration assembly and show people a pretty picture or read a story about my family. I need something imaginative. Creative. More **WOW**. No offence, but our family is really not that interesting."

The Twinzies looked insulted. Again, I ignored them.

It's usually for the best.

"Uh-huh? Well, you better start thinking then, *girrrrlfrien'*," said Mum in her best American home-girl accent, with her hands on her hips, "otherwise, you'll be trying to think of an idea until you finally reach your eleventh birthday next year! Now eat up. You need to feed that big-girl brain of yours."

"Is this one of the **ducks** we saw in the park last weekend?" asked Peter Twinzie, raising an eyebrow half in horror, half in fascinated delight at the prospect.

The Twinzies had been sizing up the duck and pancakes Mum had just put on the table.

"No, silly," said Lena Twinzie, all very matter-of-factly. "It's a frozen one from Iceland."

"Ducks can't live in Iceland, they'd be too cold… But I suppose their feathers keep them warm," said Peter.

"There's no feathers on this duck," said Lena with raised eyebrows.

"It's crispy duck!" Peter exclaimed, which made them giggle uncontrollably like he'd just said the most hilarious thing ever.

I ask you, how can anyone conjure up ideas of creative genius while living under these conditions?

I needed to remain calm. There was time to ace this. The actual assembly was near the end of term. I had around eight weeks. But Miss Peach was keen to start hearing ideas as soon as possible — and I didn't want to look like I had an empty head in front of my classmates. "Consider it easy homework," Miss Peach had said. Easy homework? Reciting all the times tables backwards would surely be easier? Ooh, an idea to add to the list — I made a mental note to jot that one down later.

The prospect of standing onstage in front of all those people, with the strong possibility of making myself look like a complete idiot, was turning me into a jittery wreck. And now Miss Peach turning this into some kind of warped homework assignment was adding to the torture.

"I don't want to do this. Who needs homework anyway? What's the point?" I muttered sulkily.

I could feel heat starting to rise in me. Knots forming in my stomach — maybe half in excitement and definitely half in fear. **Victory! Hopelessness! Victory! Hopelessness!**

My see-sawing heart flipped this-a-way and that-a-way. And Miss Peach would probably tell me off for using too many exclamation marks, because "they should only be used sparingly to express powerful emotions", but I can tell you I was feeling powerfully emotional right there and then! Whoever created homework should be shot from a cannon into the deepest part of space!! And who would even dream up the idea of working at home anyway?!! Surely that's not what homes are for!!!! **ARRGGGHHHH!!!!!**
I hate homework! Especially this homework!!!!!!!!!!

"**AHA!** Did someone mention homework?" asked my very excited dad, bounding in like a puppy after a bouncing ball.

Dad was home! Yes! He'd think of something.

I think Dad went into the wrong job. Though he's a boring accountant, anything to do with making or creating and he's on it like a car bonnet. Speaking of bonnets, I mean, literally, the Easter Bonnet Parade is a perfect example. Everyone else cuts up bits of tissue paper and sticks little eggs and bunny rabbits onto straw hats bought from the pound shop. But not us. Our bonnets are properly made from scratch. One year, Dad made me a **huge, life-size rabbit hat out of papier mâché**. It was so good, it looked like it could come to life and jump into a Muppets movie. So it's no surprise that our (Dad's) hats are widely admired at the parade every year. He's delighted that he gets to make three hats now that **the Twinzies** have started school. He's in bonnet heaven.

"Sunshine needs an idea for her school assembly but she's already spurned my idea of talking about the family, Tony, so I'm sure she can come up with something worthy of being *far* more interesting than anything we could suggest," said Mum, shutting down my hope just like that. Me and my big mouth. I mean, come on though, Mum's ideas weren't about to win any prizes.

I looked at Dad and he looked at me. By the twinkle in his eyes, I knew that victory was still within my grasp. Dad loves a challenge.

"We'll think of something," he whispered. I winked. He winked back. With Dad on the case, whatever ~~he we~~ I did was now bound to be brilliant.

6

HAWAIIAN PIZZA

There was great excitement at school the next day.

Miss Peach announced there were going to be two school discos after all the assemblies as a way of saying thank you for our efforts: one for the lower school (jelly, ice cream and orange squash, etc.) and the other for the upper school (jelly, ice cream and lemonade — leaving the fizz for the older kids, I guess).

I wasn't sure who was more excited, Miss Peach or us.

"I know you will do yourselves and the school proud," she said, clasping her hands together (but maybe the hand-clasp was more in hopeful prayer). "We want to put on **the greatest show on earth**, so that we can really let our collective hair down at the end of it!"

No pressure.

But, to my shame and absolute horror, some of my classmates were already rising to the challenge.

Izzy James said she was thinking of playing a classical piece of music to celebrate achieving her Grade 2 in piano.

Dominika Kamińska was going to break out her violin.

Carey Crick and Riley Edmunds were going to join forces and break out into a fight — well, a joint martial arts demonstration, as they attended lessons together.

Marcus Cruickshank said he was going to fly a kite, as this was an activity he enjoyed with his father. Miss Peach had to remind him that there would be no wind inside to lift it and that the dimensions of the school hall were more limited than the dimensions of the open sky. She asked him to modify his "very good idea", because the spirit of it was "**A1!**" and "**tip-top stuff**".

Poor Marcus, he couldn't catch a break. But at least he'd come up with an idea that he was willing to share — even though it was more out-there than his actual kite.

Evie was keeping her cards close to her chest, but wore a knowing smile on her lips.

"Have you decided what you're going to do for the show, Evie? Are you going to talk about your Italian holiday?" I asked her as we were going out to play at break.

Evie's eyes widened in horror. Hmph! Anyone would have thought I'd asked her to steal all the toilet rolls from Buckingham Palace.

"Ah, wouldn't you like to know?" she said, tapping at her nose like a woodpecker at a tree.

"Well...yes, I would, that's why I asked," I muttered under my breath so that she wouldn't hear.

Evie stuck her nose in the air, as if she'd heard me loud and clear after all. "You'll see," she said. Her nose was so high up in the air at this point, it could have taken flight.

"Right then, see you later," I said, before turning away and marching over to Charley and Arun in the playground.

Phwwwhttt! That was getting to be so typical of Evie — so starry and dramatic. I was determined not to be hanging on to every word she said, not like everyone else around here.

But Evie had stirred something inside of me. It was time to stop worrying and get trying, before I got left behind with Marcus Cruickshank's kite.

I needed to speak to Grandad, but it was Dad who picked up **the Twinzies** and me from school that day.

Things just didn't feel right without Grandad coming to get us, which was making me feel increasingly twitchy. I knew it had to be the weather that was stopping Grandad in his tracks. It had been a bit patchy, with sunshine and showers battling it out between themselves, so Grandad was probably finding it harder to shake off his cold. But I just wanted to be sure.

"Is Grandad okay?" I asked.

"We all have our ups and downs. But your grandad is as strong as an ox. The topsy-turvy weather hasn't helped much," said Dad.

I smiled. Just as I'd thought.

Grandad was up soon after we got home and he and **the Twinzies** went out into the garden. He said that the rest had done him "**the world of good**", and I didn't want to stop him from getting a bit of fresh air. Grandad always said "a breath of fresh air waters the soul".

Cheered by seeing Grandad up and about, I grabbed my little **Things and places of interest** notebook and got busy making a list of ideas for the assembly.

Dad was upstairs getting his "**Tony Time**", as he calls it, which meant reading his newspaper while sitting on the toilet, so there was no point in disturbing him. Besides, this was my show, and it was time to get this show on the road!

There were still two main points of concern:

Number 1 – What to do.

Number 2 – Absolutely NOT making a fool of myself in doing whatever the "what to do" was going to be.

Now I had the major principles down, the next stage was to think about what I really liked to do – and why X was important to me.

I sat in Grandad's old, beaten-down leather chair that had been in our living room since way before I was born. No one else was ever allowed to sit in Grandad's chair, apart from **the Twinzies** and me, because, according to Grandad, it was our very own magic chair and no one else but us could see how special it was. **The Twinzies** and I would take it in turns to sit in the chair — or sit on top of each other in it — and dream of the adventures we'd have when we grew up. Grandad would sit on the sofa and listen and clap as we spoke of helping to protect endangered animals and rainforests and how we would love to visit every single country in the world.

Mum had been trying to get rid of the chair for years — along with Grandad's car. I don't know why, because it was the comfiest seat **EVER**. I hoped the whiff of leather, honey and soap with a hint of aniseed, which smelled exactly like Grandad, would seep into my bones to inspire me.

I poised my pencil at my lips and kept my eyes squeezed firmly shut in readiness for the genius that would surely strike. Aha! I'd had an idea — a few ideas, in fact. My empty well was no longer dry.

✳ GYMNASTICS: Yes, my skills were quite basic, but Mum was impressed enough with my self-taught tricks to say that I could start gymnastics lessons soon. To me that was already like being given a gold medal. Simone Biles, watch out! So what if my performance would just be a series of one-handed cartwheels and walkovers. I knew that most of my class couldn't do that — and there was potential. Great idea!

✳ PLACES: Yes, my love of geography. Mum and Dad gave me a globe last Christmas and every night I spin it, close my eyes and stop it by jabbing a finger at it. Each country my finger finds, that's a country I'm going to visit when I grow up. I've started making a list. So far, the country I will visit most is Canada. Maybe it's no coincidence that my finger has landed there a lot, because it's the second-largest country in the world, but my finger has also struck on Vatican City, which is the smallest country in the world (even though it's slightly confusingly called a city, but anyway, I'm going there too!). Perhaps I could do a spinning globe-y thing on stage? Good potential.

⭐PIZZA: I could make my favourite, Hawaiian pizza, in a cookery demonstration, just like a celebrity chef. Maybe the Hawaiian is my favourite pizza of all because I like countries and places so much? Mum would probably have something to say about this as my cookery choice though. Just like her dislike for internet shopping, she thinks that putting pineapple on pizza is "a crime against humanity". So dramatic! But suppose I fascinated everyone with the fact that Hawaiian pizzas don't actually originate from Hawaii but from a Greek man who moved to Canada? Yes! Geography, cookery and clever-clogginess rolled into one. Genius!

But the more I thought about all my ideas, the more I worried about the practicalities.

GYMNASTICS: Mrs Honeyghan (probably the strictest head teacher in the universe) is the queen of health and safety, and I knew she'd try to limit me to just one or two cartwheels, in fear that I would do what had now become known as "a Marcus Cruickshank" with a death-defying plunge off the stage. Mrs Honeyghan has never quite recovered from me tripping over my smock in the school nativity and knocking Marcus, in his donkey costume, into the front row of the audience. He even "ee-awed" like a donkey as he fell.

GYMNASTICS.

PLACES: Would it really be that interesting for everyone to watch me spinning a globe around on my finger like a basketball player who loves geography?

PLACES.

PIZZA: Mrs Honeyghan and her health-and-safety fears would shut down the operation as soon as I mentioned the words "pizza oven". That, combined with Mum's pineapple pizza hatred, was a double whammy that would be hard to overcome.

PINEAPPLE PIZZA PARTY.

I'd almost forgotten about my two bonus ideas!

I still had gardening as a backup plan. I wondered if I really did have enough time to grow something for the assembly. But maybe I could take a clipping from Rose Pepper and tell everyone about my long-lost grandmother instead? But then I pictured the look that would be on Mum's face if I foghorned the details of our runaway grandmother to a packed audience.

ROSE PEPPER.

Reciting the times tables from back to front. Though a neat trick, and an obvious sign of genius, was times-table wizardry really going to get people excited? Plus, I still always got stuck on 6x8 and 11x12. And 12x11 would almost come first if I was doing the times tables backwards, so I'd fall at the first hurdle. No! Times tables were definitely STRUCK OFF THE LIST.

Oof! Back to square one.

7

THE SCREAM

Less than fifteen minutes later, I had "**an accident**".

When I say "an accident", Mum would call it "**wilful disobedience**".

"***KARIS SUNSHINE SIMPSON**, what in the name of heaven and earth have you done to yourself this time?"

Don't be fooled. This is never really a question.

If Mum calls me Sunshine, it's all good. If she calls me Karis, I'm heading downhill — fast. But if it's ***KARIS SUNSHINE SIMPSON*** — shouted in capital letters and italics for extra oomph — all fire, lightning bolts and hailstones are about to fall on my head.

It was one of those moments.

It seemed a great idea at the time.

This is what happened…

I had pulled a chair from the dining room into the living room so that I could stand on it and have a serious word with myself in the mirror that hung over the mantelpiece.

I stared hard at my horsey face, willing it into action, moving my eyebrows up and down and narrowing my eyes so that I could make my eyebrows almost meet in the middle. Did I look a little crinkled?

Then it struck me! Maybe a change in look was what I needed to turn into a new, less silly and more interesting me, who would be full of **bright ideas**. Yes! I could be sophisticated, like the people in the American shows Mum enjoys watching so much. **Sophisticated Sunny**, not **Silly Sunny** — I liked the sound of that. And what better place to start with the new proper grown-up me than with my hair!

Sometimes I wear my hair up in a single bobble on top of my head or in two buns, which I quite like. But Mum usually parts my hair in the middle and knits together three plaits on either side, like thick ropes. Mum says it's more practical to manage my hair day-to-day that way. Yes, practical, but truly boring. I needed a **spark of life**. Something different. Something with snap.

I unravelled two of my plaits and pulled the hair down over my eyes, spreading it across my nose so that it covered some of my crinkly old horse face. Perhaps a fringe would suit me if I cut it into shape, I thought.

I fell off the chair (because I'd forgotten I was standing on it), tiptoed down the hallway, quietly rifled through the kitchen drawer and found the scissors. Dad was still upstairs enjoying his "**Tony Time**" and Grandad and **the Twinzies** were still in the garden.

I returned to my position in front of the living-room mirror, snipped at the ends of my hair and let go. My hair sprang back up and away from my face. It was fun, so I took another bit of my hair and did the same thing, cutting some more off and watching it **boing** back up.

That's when Mum entered the scene. I hadn't heard her come in.

She looked tired and bedraggled after getting caught in the rain on her way home from work. It had been a tough day in the debt-advising world by the look of her — and it was about to turn into an even tougher day for me.

In one of our lessons at school, we'd looked at olden-time artists and we'd learned about an amazing painting called **The Scream** by a man called Edvard Munch. Well, that's what Mum's face reminded me of at that moment.

Her body went all tight and stiff, like she was going to shoot off into the sky, whizzing and exploding like a **firework**. In fact, she often says, **"Just light my fuse and watch me go!"** and at that very moment I knew exactly what she meant.

"Tony! Tony! Have you seen this?" she half-called, half-bellowed.

I could see Dad through the crack in the living-room door, flying down the stairs with his long legs probably taking two steps at a time, and his arms flapping wildly like a giant bird of prey.

Grandad Bobby made his way in from the back garden, panting and out of breath, with one Twinzie either side of him.

"Oh!" said Grandad and **the Twinzies** and Dad in unison.

Mum changed from tropical storm into full hurricane force on Dad. "How could you let this happen? I can't leave this house for a second without someone doing some stupidnesses!"

I'm not sure that "**stupidnesses**" is actually a word, but it wasn't the right time to point that out.

"I was only upstairs for a nanosecond," said Dad, looking a little afraid. Mum and I both raised our eyebrows at that declaration.

"Chuh! Don't be too harsh on her, Cheryl. Kids will be kids," said Grandad Bobby, trying in vain to make it better.

Mum gave Grandad her best *You dare interfere* stare, which could **freeze lemonade into a home-made ice lolly** in seconds. He had no choice but to sigh, look at me — shaking his head in pity — and return to the garden, to let Mum deal with this "terrible business".

I think Mum was so shocked, she just jumped on the phone to my godmother Patsy (Mum's best friend) and to my other grandparents to have a mega-whinge about what I'd done instead. I mean, was my hair so bad? There were short tufts at the front, where I'd done most of the cutting, and longer hair at the back. "**Peaks and troughs**", Dad had said later. It wasn't the style I was going for exactly, but at least it was different. Very different.

Anytime I tried to interject to clear my name, Mum raised her hand and said: "**Big people talking**", which in Jamaican grown-ups language means, *Adults are talking, stop interrupting — this is none of your business!* This was a bit of a cheek really, as it was me she was talking about.

So once the news was out, **the doorbell rang, and rang – and RANG. It was like church bells were ringing for a royal wedding.**

First my Granny Cynthie and Grampie Clive scuttled in, then my godmother Patsy came over after she'd finished work. Even Mrs Turner popped her head around the door. I hadn't realized how important my hair was to my family — and their friends! But then I realized something quite important. Who was I trying to kid? My hair was a mess. It was awful. I needed a miracle to make it better.

"Let the mourners come," Grandad joked, winking at me and trying to make me feel better. He caught himself as Mum's laser glare ripped through him like she was Supergirl using her eyes to cut through a sheet of glass.

Dad, Grandad Bobby and Grampie Clive kept themselves out of the way — laughing and joking in the garden. How I wished I could go out and laugh and joke with them, because inside wasn't funny — it wasn't funny at all.

Mum, Granny Cynthie, Godmother Patsy and Mrs Turner, well, they filed past my hair like they were at a funeral.

Grandad Bobby came back in to get a glass of his **"medicinal waters"**, as he calls it — Mum just calls it rum. "You're okay, my sweet Sunshine," he said. **"Worse things happen, worse things happen.** Nobody died."

"But everything's awful, Grandad. I've made my hair look stupid, I still don't know what to do for assembly, and I lost the skipping challenge at school."

"Chuh, man! Winning every time can dull the senses. When you need to reach further, life pulls

you higher. Don't worry, you'll bounce back in no time at all. Life's an adventure. There will always be twists and turns."

And just in that moment it felt like I'd been given a great big mug of hot chocolate, with gooey marshmallows, cream and chocolate sprinkles on top.

"And what has the skipping challenge got to do with cutting your hair off?" questioned Mum, hands on hips, not understanding at all. "I'll have to see if I can get you a hairdresser's appointment as soon as possible to even it out a bit."

I mean, why didn't she just make a YouTube video or tie me to the back of a plane and fly me around the world with a sign saying, **STUPID KID OVER HERE!** Talk about broadcasting your private business across the universe. Mum always says that people gossip at the hairdresser's. She says "it's a breeding ground for news — good or bad". My hair would be mud!

I didn't say all this out loud, of course; I cut off my hair, I did not remove my brain. I nodded. "Thank you, Mum," I said.

It was as if she'd picked up on some of my thoughts. Mums are scary like that. "Or maybe I should just leave it to grow back in? Honestly, what am I going to do with you, child!"

Mum's disappointment rained over the whole house. At the dinner table, she slammed down the plates a little harder than usual, and my chilli and rice virtually took flight straight into my mouth. For the rest of the evening she complained about everything and nothing in particular while trying to restyle my hair, all **"I'm fed up to the back teeth with this"** and **"I'm fed up to the back teeth with that"**. Mum's poor back teeth must have been exhausted.

Mum said my punishment wasn't any more severe than sending me to bed early and not being able to use my tablet for a whole week because, "how you've massacred your hair is punishment enough and I hope you learn from this sorry episode."

The trouble is, I don't so much have episodes of trouble, it's more like a whole series.

8

CROCODILE SMILE

In hindsight — like, the next morning — the realization that it probably wasn't the greatest move to slice and dice my hair behind Mum's back sank in.

After combing my hair this way and that way, which made my eyes water, Mum had finally settled on parting the front into small sections and then putting it into single bobbles so that it looked like I had **little palm trees** or a **majestic crown** on my head. The back of my hair, which I hadn't cut, was put into a bun. Maybe my hair wasn't so bad after all. I thought it looked quite stylish, actually. Mum really had performed a miracle! Even so, I decided it was best to keep a low profile — I didn't know how my classmates might react. That's the thing about change, everyone seems to have an opinion on it. And I didn't want to be accused of trying to be the centre of attention — again.

Being discreet was easier said than done when you were walking to school with Grandad Bobby, one of the most famous people in the world. He was probably more famous than really famous people like the prime minister or Beyoncé — at least where we live.

Grandad always stood out in a crowd. Aside from looking like a little ox with his broad shoulders and short, sturdy legs, everyone recognized Grandad for his hats.

Grandad owned lots of pork-pie hats in different styles. The hats are obviously not made from real pork pies — they are kind of pinched at the top with a narrow brim, I suppose a bit like a pork pie. His favourite and most elaborate hat was made from straw, with a brown silk ribbon wrapped around it and three colourful feathers poking out from the ribbon.

When I was younger, I said to Grandad that he should audition to be Father Christmas if anything ever happened to the real one, because he'd be perfect for the job, with his fuzzy white beard, round tummy and big, deep laugh. I told him he could keep his hat.

"**A Jamaican Father Christmas at the North Pole with a pork-pie hat?** Now wouldn't that be something! I'd make sure to pack my thermal socks and long johns," he laughed.

We always left for school extra early to accommodate Grandad's cheery hellos or being stopped by people in the street to have "**a little chat**". That morning, I could only be grateful that **the Twinzies** drew attention away from me with their gap-toothed, six-and-sweet Twinzie cuteness. Peter Twinzie, with his mini, perfectly rounded afro, and Lena Twinzie, with her four pigtails — two at the front and two at the back of her head — are instantly munchable and a brilliant diversion tactic.

Mr Chanda at Chanda's Groceries waved; so did Mrs Flowers the florist and Jakub at the Polski Sklep, as well as Mrs Turner — though Grandad always made his best attempts to hurry past her.

"Chuh, man! She chats for too long," Grandad would say. But Mrs Turner always managed to catch him on his way back home and ask him to do her **"little jobs"**, meaning Grandad staying with her for hours. Mum says that since her husband "mysteriously walked out one day with his suitcase and never came back", Mrs T gets lonely. More to the point, I think she was crushing on Grandad. **YUCK!**

Even with the distraction of **the Twinzies** and my random thoughts, I was still feeling self-conscious about my new hair as we walked. But it was as if Grandad knew what I was thinking about, because he suddenly said, "If people were all the same, my sweet Sunshine, the world would be a far less interesting place. **It's good to celebrate and to learn from difference.** Helps make the world turn."

Grandad Bobby came to England from Jamaica in the 1950s, a long time before Mum and Auntie Sharon were

born. Grandad says that when he first arrived and started driving buses for a living, he had to learn about the English way of life very quickly. It was some of the simple things he found most odd — like people **eating fish and chips out of newspapers**, **bottles of milk being left by a milkman** on the doorstep, and people carrying unwrapped loaves of bread home from the bakers under their armpits (**sweaty bread — ugh! Yuck!**).

"Don't you worry about a thing," said Grandad. "**You have beautiful hair.**"

I smiled. Grandad always knew what to say. But as we drew nearer to school, I started to feel increasingly nervous.

I hung back, my footsteps becoming so slow that eventually Grandad and the Twinzies disappeared around the corner.

By the time I rounded it after them, Grandad was leaning against the trunk of an old willow tree, with his head hanging down, holding his side. **The Twinzies** ran around the tree, chasing each other, not noticing anything peculiar.

I have a vivid imagination at the best of times, but the

tree looked like it was bending to scoop Grandad up and hold him in its arms — I mean, its branches. A little shiver ran down my spine.

"Are you okay, Grandad?" I asked.

"Yes, mi all right," he said, sounding a little out of breath. But then he smiled. "Mi just waiting for an old slowcoach. Hurry now, or we'll be late." He gently took hold of my hand and squeezed it. "Sometimes it's better to face what you most dread out in the open. You can't stay hiding in a corner for ever, the spiders and mice might get you!"

I laughed and held Grandad's hand a bit tighter.

"Come on," he said. *"We'll do this together. What mi always tell you? Life's an adventure!"*

There was no chance to hide or run or do anything else anyway then, because, as our feet hit the playground, Charley and Arun rushed towards us.

"Oh, your hair's different," said Arun, coming to a sudden, dramatic standstill, with his eyes wide open and mouth pinched, as if he was working out whether he liked my new style or not. "I love it! It's quirky, just like you!"

"Yes," said Charley, confirming Arun's thoughts. "It looks really, really cool!"

I grinned broadly. See, what do big people know anyway? I love my friends!

"Thanks, guys. You always have my back," I said.

"How can we have your back when we're standing right in front of you?" Charley winked.

I laughed and Arun shook his head at Charley's rubbish joke. "You're the best," I cheered and hugged her.

I have known Charley and Arun for ever and ever, amen.

Charley and I were instant friends from nursery after we both said we had **horses as pets** (don't ask, but — just for clarification — we don't) and now Mum and Charley's mum are friends too. Charley has bright red hair cut into a sharp, neat bob, and blue eyes the size of the sky. If Charley was an animal, I think she'd be a **kitten**. Her voice is like the sweetest **miaow** and you just want to protect her. Mum says Charley is "**delightful**". She is! If there was a kindest-girl-in-the-world championship, I know Charley would win hands-down every time. But she's also like a wise old owl.

A kitten–owl: innocent but knowing.

We became friends with Arun on that day too, when he said that our horses looked like **dragons**. Realizing that neither a horse nor a dragon would make it in the accuracy department, Charley and me changed our tune and told our nursery teacher, Mrs Christie, that the dragon-horses were big dogs instead. We don't have dogs either, but it sounded more realistic. Charley, Arun and I shook hands on that idea, nodding in agreement and sealing our friendship since that day. **Always and for ever!**

Arun's warm brown face has a mop of shiny dark hair, with a long fringe that looks like a huge wave sweeping across the top of it. And the way he blows upwards from his top lip and then brushes the hair away from his eyes is **sooo** cute. Mum says that Arun has "**movie-star looks**". Mum's right. Arun is so amazing and he doesn't even know it. Whenever anyone pays him a compliment, he scrunches his face like he's just eaten something bitter, glows red and waves you away, along with the compliment.

Anyway, I'm getting distracted. The main thing was my friends weren't worried about my hair. Instead, they turned excitedly to Grandad. **"Can you teach us a new song**, Grandad Bobby, can you?" asked Charley. "We haven't heard one in ages."

Charley and Arun enjoy nothing better than a good sing-song — especially all the ancient stuff. It's like they're old before their time. Grandad used to sing traditional Caribbean songs in the playground for us — and then sometimes break out into a dance routine for good measure. I was embarrassed at first. But everyone seemed to enjoy **Grandad's songs, raps and poems** — and I had to take it on the chin that my grandad was actually cooler than me!

Hey...maybe my hope for the celebration assembly lay in Grandad? He could make a song and dance out of someone's old, smelly socks. But then he couldn't go onstage for me, could he? How I wished I was more like him. Grandad always wore who he was and where he came from with pride.

Grandad would always tell us that, **"Your history is what helps to make you who you are."**

Mum said to me once that she was embarrassed by Grandad's ways when she was younger. "All I wanted when I was your age, Sunshine, was to fit in. To look like and be like the other kids around me, so that I could melt into the background. I didn't want to stand out or be different. But my culture and skin colour *was* different to that of the other kids I knew at school. I didn't pay any attention to your grandad for many years, but then one day I realized he was right. **I had to embrace who I was.**"

It's like she's been catching up ever since, because all we hear about is **"Olaudah Equiano was a former slave who campaigned to abolish slavery"** this and **"Barack Obama was the first black American President"** that. **Blah, blah, blah.** I mean, I'm sure this information is interesting when you're one hundred years old, or like thirty or something, but not when you're my age.

For a moment I thought that maybe these were topics I could talk about for the assembly...but history is so boring.

My mind drifted to thinking about Evie. If only I had a glamorous holiday story to share like she did about meeting George Pooley in Italy. Now that would be a-mazing.

Where was Evie anyway? I looked around the

playground but couldn't spot her. We'd all usually be standing together, with her dad catching up with Grandad. Maybe she was in a mood with me from the day before? We hadn't spoken since our little "**incident**" over what she was going to do at the assembly. If whatever Evie was planning was so **top-secret**, it was bound to be something special. But who cared what she was going to do? I knew I could do something better.

Maybe. Or maybe not.

I caught myself gulping down a huge ball of air. A ball of air that felt like fright.

Grandad was laughing with Charley and Arun. "Hey, hey, mi too tired to teach you a new song this morning, but how about mi share a little poem with you. Gather round and let me tell you about **Moses Supposes**."

We all huddled, parents included.

Grandad Bobby whispered the words quickly, but Grandad's whispers sounded a bit like someone's normal speaking voice, except a bit louder, so his words rose up above our little scrum like steam whistling out of a boiling kettle.

"Moses supposes his toeses are roses,
But Moses supposes erroneously.
For nobody's toeses are roses or posies,
As Moses supposes his toeses to be.
For Moses he knowses his toeses aren't roses,
As Moses supposes his toeses to be!"

Grandad said the same words again and again, getting faster and faster each time, before making a mistake. Everyone laughed, because it was such a silly poem.

"What does it even mean?" asked Charley, still giggling but looking a little puzzled.

"It doesn't matter what it means," said Arun. "It's a nonsensical English rhyme." We all looked puzzled then. "It's a **tongue-twister**, a bit like '**She sells seashells on the seashore**' — get it? And the verse is also featured in the film *Singin' in the Rain* with Gene Kelly, Debbie Reynolds and Donald O'Connor."

"O-kaaay," Charley and me said together, now extremely confused, but admiring Arun's in-depth knowledge of musicals at the same time.

"What? It's one of my favourite films." Arun folded his

arms across his chest and looked a little flushed.

"That's right, Arun, you tell them. Mine too, mine too!" laughed Grandad.

Just then, the familiar sound of the school bell rang out. I'd almost forgotten where we were. And that's when I spotted her looking over at me.

The sun was out, and I squinted into the brightness. Despite the warmth in the air, I froze. Evie was standing not too far away from us, over by the entrance with her dad. She waved. Her eyes narrowed and she smiled the broadest, shiniest smile ever. Just like a crocodile, eyeing up its prey.

I forced myself to break free from Evie's gaze, turning away from her. Why was she looking at me like that?

Reflecting back on it now, I should have realized why, sooner. **Silly, silly me.**

9

UNICORNS

In class, the morning had started out lovely.

I was in a group with Arun and Charley, **creating pictures of different foods from around the world**. Evie was placed in another group with Izzy James and Maya Watkins. I wondered if Evie had asked Miss Peach to team her up with someone else. Maybe that's what the funny look in the playground had been about? She was telling me without telling me that she'd moved on. Maybe I wasn't good enough for Evie's sophisticated tastes? Or maybe she just didn't need me any more? She had well and truly made her mark on the school by now, anyway. But then again, maybe she'd told Miss Peach that I hadn't been very helpful to her. Useless even.

I didn't hang out with Izzy and Maya much, but they were nice enough, and perhaps they'd be better friends than me? I scratched at my neck and forehead, suddenly feeling very hot and itchy, guilt flaring up inside of me.

But I had to admit, as much as I didn't want to claim the title of **Worst Friend in the World**, it was nice to feel free again. The responsibility of being Evie's class buddy had weighed heavily on my shoulders. Making sure she knew where everything was when she first started at school. Making sure she was happy. Making sure I didn't take offence at practically everything she said to me. Or maybe that was just an allergic reaction to all her perfectness?

I mean, she's so perfectly delicate and dainty too, while I have scrapes and bruises on my elbows and knees from where I bash them when playing. It's like she floats on a **cloud** or rolls around in cotton wool all day. Being around her just makes me feel like a clumsy wreck.

Maybe Miss Peach had special powers and picked up

with her **witchy senses that there was toil and trouble stirring between us**, and decided to let me off the hook from being with Evie?

Whatever it was, I felt okay about it, I decided. Until a little piece of paper hit me on the head. I turned around. Evie put her hand to her mouth in a yawning motion and made a pouty face. I think she was telling me she was bored. She could have fooled me! She, Izzy and Maya had been giggling together for most of the lesson, like they were keeping exciting secrets.

I smiled back at Evie, guilty prongs beginning to jab at my insides again that I'd been grateful to get away from her in the first place. "I'll speak to you later," I mouthed and turned back into my comfortable blanket of happiness with Arun and Charley.

"School is much more fun when I'm with you," said Evie, still pouting, on our way out for break.

"I'm sure Miss Peach is just trying to get you involved with everyone else now that you've been here nearly a whole year. You'll be fine. You're doing just great." I smiled. I meant it, she *was* doing great. Perhaps too great.

Evie smiled back. "Erm, Sunny, did you go to the hairdresser's last night?"

My hand flew up to my hair. "No, I had a bit of a home trim." It wasn't a lie.

Evie laughed. "Oh, I can tell! I thought you'd actually paid for someone to do it." Evie put her hand up to her chin and looked closely at my hair. "Hmm...it's fine...**it just looks a little...a little ishy**, that's all. Stumpy. Your hair at the front looks a bit like a load of **unicorn horns** that have been chopped off. Hey, I wonder what you call a group of unicorns? We could christen your hairstyle with the name! Aww, you're still really cute though." Evie laughed again. She probably thought she was laughing with me.

I looked straight into her large, luminous eyes. "They're called a **blessing**," I told her, defiantly hiding my hurt. She looked at me questioningly.

"A group of unicorns is called a blessing," I confirmed. It's a random fact I've picked up along the way.

Evie's eyes narrowed coolly, but she put one arm around my shoulders warmly. "I guess that means you *are* a blessing then. **Silly Sunny** — how did you know that? Come on, let's go and catch up with the others. What should we play?"

I knew, in that moment, I just had to come up with something that would be better than whatever Evie was going to do at the Golden Jubilee assembly. I had to beat her — even though it wasn't a competition. Yeah, right. Just like the skipping challenge wasn't a competition either!

I was fed up with being **Silly Sunny**. It was time to say goodbye to the old me and say hello to a **brand-new, shiny, perfect me**.

10

COCKEREL HEAD

Mum had a word in my ear that evening, because she caught me looking in the living-room mirror and messing with my hair again when she got home from work.

Her face stiffened when she saw me. To her it must have been a playback of the day before. Although then she'd looked like she'd walked in to see me being mauled by a lion.

"Sunny, what's wrong?"

I sighed deeply and then pulled at one of my chopped-off unicorn horns. "Does my hair look really terrible, Mum? Do I have the worst hair in the world? Will I be laughed at for ever?" I said, sounding not at all over-the-top.

Mum's face softened. She sat down and patted the sofa, which I guessed was her code for *Sit down, I'm about to give you a lecture you won't forget*.

"You must never *ever* think that, or that anyone is better than you; big hair, short hair, long hair, no hair — it doesn't matter. **We are all different**," said Mum.

"Does my hair look a bit ishy though?"

"**Ishy?** What does that mean?" Mum asked with arched eyebrows.

"I guess, it's just there, hanging around and not very interesting," I said.

Mum and Dad are just ordinary parents who do really parenty things like bossing us about, telling us what to do all the time and making sure we're fed and watered, blah, blah, blah. And, yes, they are boring because they are very sensible people, but, crucially, being so sensible, they do occasionally give good advice — even though they go on a bit.

Mum's eyebrows arched to new heights. "Go on," she said. "Why do you think that? Why do you think your hair is '**ishy**'? I'm interested to hear."

I took a deep breath and told Mum about what had happened at school and being told I looked like a gone-wrong unicorn. But I didn't tell her that it was Evie who had said those words.

"Who said that to you?" asked Mum.

I said nothing. I don't know why. An honour thing: kids versus parents, I suppose. Never tell. Tell and you're asking for trouble. There'll be question after question.

"I asked you a question, young lady. Who said it?"

"EVIE EVANS!"

That didn't take long. Trust me, when you're called **"young lady"** in that stern way, you better 'fess up everything quick.

Mum's brow furrowed as she digested this bit of info.

"Evie? Evie in your class? Your friend Evie?"

I nodded.

"Did you tell your teacher?"

"No, Mum."

"Why not?"

"It didn't seem important."

"Hmm. You like school, don't you, Sunny?"

"Yes, Mum. Usually."

"Usually?"

"Most of the time. It's just a bit awkward with Evie at the moment."

"What do you mean, awkward?"

Silence.

"Hmm. Shame. It's a shame. A real shame," said Mum.

There was a long pause as Mum waited for me to speak.

"Did you say something to upset her?" she asked, finally giving up on the waiting.

WHY WAS THIS MY FAULT? EVERYTHING WAS ALWAYS MY FAULT.

I folded my arms.

Mum knew that the dial on my offended-ometer was very, very high. "What I mean is, Sunny, has something happened to spoil your friendship?"

I clamped shut again. To be honest, I didn't know what was happening. I couldn't put my finger on it, but I was starting to feel smaller, as if I was shrinking.

Mum tried a different route.

"What about Charley and Arun?"

A smile made a comeback to my face. "Yes, Charley and Arun are my best friends."

Mum smiled.

At this point she could have given me a hug and been done with it. But Mum is not really a hugger. She shows her devotion in other ways, like cooking us nutritious food when we'd rather have chips and talking us to death.

One time I poured her "**delicious**" cauliflower soup into a plant pot when she wasn't looking. A few days later the plant died. I had a lucky escape, I reckon. But I did feel bad about the plant. Mum thought it had developed some terrible algae-like disease. I'd kept my mouth shut. But that was then and this was now.

Mum nodded and tipped her head to the side thoughtfully. I knew what this meant. She was about to properly go off on one of her long, rambling lectures.

"Sometimes, people can say or do things that they don't really mean without properly thinking it through. And then cause harm without realizing what they've done."

Mum adjusted the cushions, making herself extra comfortable to tell her story.

"I was the only Black child in my class in primary school. One day, one of my plaits unravelled," she began. "My teacher, Mrs Jones, who I loved, told me she was sorry but she couldn't help me because she didn't know how to re-plait it. She didn't even want to touch it. It was my misfortune that this happened just before morning break, so I had to walk around with my hair sticking up in all kinds of directions all day and the other kids wouldn't stop teasing me. They called me '**cockerel head**', which is quite funny, I suppose — but not if the joke is aimed at you."

I guess that was one of the reasons Mum reacted so badly when I cut my hair off. Poor Mum, she must have stuck out like a sore thumb when she was at school.

Mum is tiny, **like a miniature doll**, with a small face and a little pointed chin, like an upside-down teardrop, and her hair is always extremely neat: swept upwards and out of the way in a tight ballerina's bun. Jamaicans would say my mum is "**likkle but tallawah**", meaning that she is small, but strong and fearless. And she is, but in a quiet, serious

98

way. So to look at her now, and see how tall and proud she stands — in character, not in height — I can't believe she got picked on at school.

"The point is, Sunny, people can be unkind, but I can assure you, hair or no hair, you are beautiful, funny, warm and precious. Yes, Evie has lovely hair, but so do you, if that is what this is about. That's one of the amazing things about being Black, we can do so many sassy things with our hair types. We are individuals and that's what makes all of us special in our own way — tight curls, loose curls or no curls. The only thing "**ish**" about you should be in your **swish**, sweetie. Move with confidence in your steps."

I smiled and nodded.

"**Just lay off the scissors** and leave it to a professional hair stylist, is all that I would recommend. Okay?" Mum smiled.

I smiled a little more. "Okay, Mum."

I can't imagine being the only Black kid in school and standing out like that. There are loads of kids whose families come from different parts of the world at my school — Poland, Ghana, Nigeria, Grenada, India, Pakistan,

Bangladesh — and, of course, Jamaica, where my family is from.

As well as my globe, I've also got a big map of the world in my room that covers the wall right behind my bed. **Every time I meet someone new, I find their country and stick a yellow dot on it.** My goal is for the map to get covered in sunshine-yellow dots. I'm very busy with my map and my globe.

Mum cocked her head to the other side, which meant another story was brewing. Whatever she was about to say, I knew it would probably end up with her talking about **Martin Luther King**.

Dr Martin Luther King Jr stood up for Black people in America a long time ago, just like **Malcolm X**. Black people weren't allowed to go into the same places as white people, like restaurants, or go to the same schools (they had to go to separate "**coloured**" schools), or use the same toilets, or water fountains to have a drink when they were thirsty, or anything. And then a lot of people worked together — in what they called the civil rights movement — to campaign for Black people to be given the same rights as white people. Because, you know, we are humans too. My blood bleeds red, not green or blue.

Mum and Dad love to talk to us about the civil rights movement because they say **"It shows how ordinary people can come together to do extraordinary things"**.

"A lot of people fought for the things we can take for granted now," said Mum. "You know in Bristol, in the 1960s, a bus company wouldn't give Black or Asian people jobs. A man called **Paul Stephenson** joined together with others to lead a boycott against the company. Thousands of people supported the boycott and the news of racism made headlines. And the bus company was eventually forced to change and lift their colour ban. Now that's people power right there."

"Grandad worked on the buses. There are still people we pass in the street who remember him and say hello," I said. "I don't understand why it was like that in the past."

"It's a hard one," said Mum. "Sometimes it feels like we go around in circles. Different countries fight each other, but then people living in the same countries can fight each other too; different religions fight each other, and people of the same religion can fight each other; different ethnicities fight each other, and people of the same ethnicity can fight each other. It's funny how prejudice can change its form but somehow stay the same."

I tried to digest Mum's words. "So what you're saying is that everyone in the world hates each other?" I imagined that I was watching the world from space as it grew bigger and bigger as it filled with so much anger, until eventually it exploded. A bit like when Bruce Banner bursts out of his clothes and turns into the Incredible Hulk.

"Not everyone feels that way, Sunny. And hate is a powerful word to use. Although some people don't get on with each other, there are still many people who do. People are people and people will always need people, whether we like it or not. It's frustrating to feel that we go around in circles, but I'm hopeful things are changing bit by bit — even though it's taken a few centuries to get there." She sighed, but smiled.

"So why doesn't everyone who doesn't like each other just get together in one big place like…I don't know…like an Olympic stadium and sort it out then?"

Mum laughed. "Well, I think we'd have to find a place a bit bigger than even the Olympics for that to happen. In truth, I think we make life more complicated than it needs to be. And that's one thing we probably do all have in common."

Then I asked her the question that is usually like **throwing a stick of dynamite into the room**.

"What about Grandma Pepper, Mum? Do you hate... I mean...dislike her?"

Mum scratched nervously at her neck. "It's even more complicated with your grandmother. **Sometimes life isn't straightforward and not a simple case of black or white.**"

I had no idea whether Mum had answered my question or not. Grown-ups can do that sometimes: they bamboozle you with puzzling answers. What did being Black or white have to do with anything? Both Mum and her mum are Black. But then, as Mum says, people of the same colour or ethnicity can dislike each other too. I don't know — why are people so people-like?

"Do you think it would be wrong to hate Evie Evans,

Mum?" I was hoping for a simple response that wouldn't take another ten minutes to answer.

"You're very young to feel that you hate anyone, Sunshine, but it can be easy to fall out with people, whatever your age. **Shall I have a word with your teacher?**"

"NOOOO! DON'T DO THAT!" I bellowed.

Mum at least saw the funny side. She laughed.

"Okay, I'll set you a challenge. Why don't you work out your niggles with Evie? She probably still has a few new-girl nerves, that's all. Set yourself that goal."

Then Mum held my face between her hands. "If I could go back in time, I'd change some of the things I said and did, but hindsight is a wonderful thing." Mum smiled. "**It took me a long while to get used to being me, Sunny.** Some people say our skin is too dark, our lips too big and our hair too woolly, but then at the same time people copy our creativity: our music, our dance, our vocabulary — even the brownness of our skin, by tanning on the beach. And I've told you how many pretty hairstyles you can create with that head-top of yours. You have nothing to prove to anyone. Unfortunately, life can sometimes make you feel like you have everything to prove. But please, don't let anyone ever tell you they are better than you. And most of all, don't believe them if they do, whether they say it out loud or not. You, your brother and sister are strong towers — and never, *ever* let anyone tear you down. You know what Dr King said?"

I answered cautiously: "Erm... 'I have a dream'?"

Mum smiled. "Yes, he did, but he also said, **'You will change your mind; you will change your looks; you will change your smile, laugh, and ways, but no matter what you change, you will always be you.'** Don't look down, Sunny. Never look down. Look up. Hold your head high. Just be the best person you can be — no matter what anyone else around you is doing. You have so much to give."

I didn't know whether to give Mum a round of applause or cry a little, because she still had a very strong grip on my face. But how could I explain to Mum that sometimes I don't want to hold my head up high? Sometimes I just want to hide down low.

And how can you not compare yourself to other

people? Everyone does that, don't they? Especially when they do things better than you can do. Life is just one big judging fest! It's exhausting.

Then I thought about all the eyes that would be gawping at me during the celebration assembly. Looking. Peering. Maybe even laughing. Laughing *at* me, not with me.

"Do you think I'm interesting, Mum or just really silly?" I casually (bluntly) slipped into the conversation.

Mum's eyes widened like I wasn't being serious. When she realized that I was, she gave a little smile.

"Sunshine, you're one of the most interesting people I've ever met. In fact, if you reined back on the interesting factor by a few notches I think we'd all sleep a little easier at night. **And there's nothing wrong with a bit of silliness** — within reason, of course." Mum's smile spread across her face.

Maybe she was thinking about the time I jumped into the deep end at the pool during my second swimming lesson because I thought I was **a mermaid**, and then sank. Or when I slid down our freshly painted banister and ended up with a white stripe running down the middle of my body — not to mention my hands and one side of my face. But then, maybe she wasn't thinking about those examples at all, because I seem to recall she wasn't smiling very much at the time.

Right there and then, I smiled back at Mum, but deep down I knew she was only trying to make me feel better — because, although she's naggy and talks a lot about boring history stuff, she's still my mum. I wanted to make her proud of me. I wanted all of my family to be proud of me, instead of always letting them down with my silliness. But how could I make them proud if I wasn't even proud of myself?

I realized then that I didn't need Evie to come in and beat me. I was doing a good job of that all on my own.

11

SHINE LIKE DIAMONDS

I think Mum must have started having secret **"big people"** discussions about **"the kids"** because, all that weekend, Dad and Grandad gave me pep talks in their own special ways. Mum knew that triggering **Operation Grandad**, in particular, was the way to get me listening.

Dad strutted across the living room, making silly poses and pretending to have his photo taken. "Ever heard of **Fanny Eaton**?" he asked. I shook my head. "Well, she may be the first Black supermodel — and one of the first supermodels ever! She made a name for herself in the 1800s, as an artist's model in Pre-Raphaelite paintings, sketches and prints — and think about all the famous Black supermodels we've had since."

I looked at Dad blankly.

"Iman, Naomi Campbell, Tyra Banks, Alek Wek?" he asked.

"I guess I've heard of some of them. Maybe. Erm, I don't mean to be rude, Dad, but is there a point to you telling me about these nice old ladies?"

"Hey, less of the old! They're some of the most beautiful and striking women ever to walk the face of the earth, and you are just as gorgeous," he said, kissing my forehead. But he would say that, because he's my dad.

Grandad Bobby said, "You're a Nubian queen, my Sunshine. But be wary of beauty. You may have eyes that shine like diamonds and lips as red as rubies, but no amount of beauty on the outside can make up for a rusting heart. The heart and the brain are the most precious things of all."

Who knows what big people are going on about half the time? If I looked like a supermodel or like Evie Evans, with all her confidence and swagger, I'd have everyone falling at my feet — instead of me being the one who's always falling over.

I told Grandad Bobby about some of the things Evie had said.

"Why you na tell your teacher?" he asked.

"No, Grandad, I'm no snitch!"

He shook his head. "**Na be afraid to talk the truth.** It doesn't matter what other people think. And you know what? **If you spit at the sky, it has a tendency to fall back in your face.**"

"But nothing ever falls or splats in Evie's face, Grandad. Not like it always does with me. She even stood up in front of the whole class and told us about this super-amazing summer holiday she had in Italy, where she met this famous actor man called **George Gooney.** I couldn't stand up in front of everyone and tie my own shoelaces."

Grandad studied my face closely.

I kept talking. "And everything I do or say ends up being wrong or silly. And everything about me is just so boring. Does my hair look terrible, do you think? And—"

"Come here, Sunshine."

Grandad held me close and then felt my forehead with one of his giant ham hands.

"Open your mouth wide and say **arrggh**."

I did as I was told. Grandad was the doctor diagnosing his patient.

"I see, I see," he said thoughtfully.

"What do you see?" I asked, sounding slightly panicked, but still knowing, whatever it was, Grandad could fix it.

"You've got a slight case of lost-voice-itis — that's all. Nothing serious."

I coughed dramatically. "I don't feel ill."

Grandad smiled. "You're not ill. It's growing pains. We all go through it. And you've had your confidence knocked here and there. You are just finding your voice, Sunshine. Finding who you are. And you *will* find your way. You're just at the beginning of you."

I didn't really want to be at the beginning of me. I wanted to be somewhere near the middle and far away from the end.

"I'm just not very good at things, Grandad. I hate

speaking in front of people because I just know I'm going to make a mistake or do something silly. I'm scared about the Golden Jubilee assembly — and, besides, I have nothing to say. I made a list, to add to the gardening idea, but it ended up being a load of rubbish. I'll bore everyone to death. I just thought that maybe if I **looked** different, then I would **be** different."

I wasn't sure if I was making any sense.

Grandad shook his head. "**As you grow, you get stronger — just look at my runner beans**. We water them, feed them, protect them from the elements the best we can, yes, and they find their way. They do their thing — and then arrive, flowering beautifully. **You'll find your way**."

I don't think the look on my face was convincing Grandad that the message was sinking in.

"You're very talented, Sunshine. Look at the way you love your English and your maths and your geography. Remember, **Katherine Johnson**, **Dorothy Vaughan** and **Mary Jackson** helped win the race to space, and **Margaret Busby** was a pioneer in publishing **books**. These women fought against the odds. If they can do it, you can do it too. There is no doubt in my mind about that. See your life as an adventure. It's yours to live, so live it the best way you can. Do your thing and don't hesitate. Go for it! And if you fall down, get up and go again."

I nodded more confidently.

"That's my girl. Don't worry about a thing, because **everything GWARN BE ALL RIGHT!**" said Grandad emphatically.

"Okay, Grandad." I smiled.

I don't think I understood all of what Grandad was saying at the time, but I did know that with him, every little thing did feel all right.

12

RED PANTS

That Sunday afternoon, my Auntie Sharon paid us a visit. She became very excited when Mum and Dad got me to tell her about the Golden Jubilee assembly. She lifted my hands and waved them around in the air while she sang a song about us being champions by some old band called **King** — or is it **Queen**? I can never remember.

Auntie Sharon has all the flair of my Grandma Pepper but, unfortunately, not the singing voice.

"It isn't a competition, Auntie Sharon," I said, trying to play down the whole, grand **fifty-year-jubilee**-thing. "It's just a boring old school assembly."

"Don't let 'em fool you," came Auntie Sharon's reply.

She tapped her nose. "This world is a stage, niecey-weesey, and we are the players. *We* are the players. Just ask old Mr Shakespeare. I'll be there with my bells and whistles, cheering you on."

That wasn't just an expression or a threat — she meant it. If Auntie Sharon ever gives up her job working at the local council, she would do well auditioning for the position of Town Crier.

I haven't introduced you to Auntie Sharon yet because she takes quite a bit of explaining, and I had to get into my flow before giving her the description she deserves.

You don't see Auntie Sharon for ages and then suddenly she appears, like bees in summertime. She's like a swarm all on her own, covering us in an abundance of kisses and leaving us bathed in the scent of her floral perfume. My Auntie Sharon is great.

She always turns up in a taxi and leaves in one as well. "Like someone out of a soap opera," Dad always says.

"Chuh!" said Grandad Bobby once. "Sharon would tek a taxi to go to the toilet."

Mum and Auntie Sharon are opposites. Yes, like chalk and

cheese, chocolate and scrambled eggs, diamonds and dust.

Auntie Sharon is **loud** in every way. Her clothes are **bright** and her hair is always styled differently, as if her head is constantly bored and needs the change. If you see someone in the street with bright yellow braids balanced on top of their head like an intricately-plaited pineapple, or a short and green close-crop, with a red fringe like a licking flame sweeping across their face, then that's probably Auntie Sharon you've spotted walking by. Although it's difficult to know what you'd see first — her colourful locks or her wobbling bottom desperately trying to break free from her skintight skirt or trousers.

Today, Auntie Sharon sported a wig of shoulder-length light-blue hair, designer-ripped skinny blue jeans, a denim top tied into a knot at the waist, and denim high-heeled shoes — with two strokes of midnight-blue lipstick kissing her lips to tie the look together.

"Only you could dare to wear triple denim and get away with it," said Dad.

"She different," said Granny Cynthie, shaking her head but smiling at the same time.

"Just like our mum. All fur coat and no knickers," Mum grumbled under her breath. I was shocked when I first heard Mum say that, and I realized way afterwards that she meant that Grandma Pepper and Auntie Sharon think more about what's stylish on the surface than about the quality of what's underneath, which I don't think is true. Mum was just being very grumpy, which she can be when it comes to her mother and her sister.

What really irritates Mum about Auntie Sharon is that whenever I spend any time with her, she always buys me new clothes. You're probably thinking what a kind auntie she is, and you're right. It's what goes with the clothes-buying that really gets on Mum's nerves.

I'll go to Auntie Sharon's house in one outfit and come back in another.

"Uh-uh, I'm not taking you out for the day dressed like that," she'll say, tutting and shaking her head disapprovingly. **"The top doesn't even match the shoes. You need fresh garms."** And then she'll take me clothes shopping and kit me out head to toe in new top, jeans and trainers — the glitzier the better! The **"old"** outfit, that

Mum put me in in the first place, will come back stuffed in a carrier bag like it's ready for the dustbin.

Mum's face sours like gone-off milk every time Auntie Sharon does it. "Don't pay any attention," Dad says, "she just likes to spoil Sunny."

Auntie Sharon doesn't live that far away from us, but there tends to be a bit of a gap between her visits, to give Mum a chance to recover. So **the Twinzies** and I mainly go to visit her now. Dad usually does the picking up and dropping off.

Oh, I've almost forgotten to mention my cousin, Auntie Sharon's son, Dariuszkz. He was visiting today too. Dariuszkz's name is pronounced **"Da-rye-us"**, but is spelled with a **"zkz"** at the end because Auntie Sharon thought it looked **"pizazzy"**. Mum says the spelling is **"plain stupid"**.

Dariuszkz hasn't really said much since he became a teenager. He's fifteen now. He just stares at his phone most of the time and mumbles when one of the grown-ups asks him a question. Mind you, with Auntie Sharon as his mum, there's not much left to say.

The only time I realize Dariuszkz is there is when I fall over his size eleven trainers as he slouches his body all over our sofa with his giraffe legs sticking out in front of him. Mind you, I can talk, I was wearing size one shoes by the time I was five.

"You all right, Daddy?" Auntie Sharon asked Grandad. "I've bought you some new garms. Get rid of some of that old frumpiness you have in your wardrobe and style you up a bit."

"Mi all right," said Grandad Bobby. "I have my own style. Besides, I came into this world without clothes and I doubt I'll need any when I leave it either."

Auntie Sharon released such a high-pitched laugh that I thought it might break the drinks glasses that were on the coffee table. She tossed her blue tresses. "You're a joker, Daddy. You'll live for ever. I like to spoil you, that's all."

"Sharon, your heart is big enough, but don't place your basket higher than where you can reach it. Especially when you don't need to."

"And what is that supposed to mean?" asked Auntie Sharon.

"I mean, look after yourself and don't spend unnecessarily. You don't have to worry about me." Grandad smiled.

Auntie Sharon and Mum both sucked their cheeks in and pursed their lips, like they'd just eaten a bag of sour sherbets in one go. I think that one of them agreed with Grandad Bobby and the other did not.

"I just want to make sure you're okay, Daddy... Have we had the results back yet?" Auntie Sharon whispered to Mum and Dad, with her teeth gritted like a terrible ventriloquist. Well, when I say whispered, I mean Auntie Sharon spoke in what other people would call a normal speaking voice.

What results? I didn't know Grandad had been taking any exams. I looked over at Mum. Her neck was stiff and her eyes started to twitch and wink as if she was a malfunctioning robot. All that was missing was smoke coming out of her ears and her head flipping back and forth on its hinges.

She was obviously trying to tell Auntie Sharon to shut up through some weird form of mime. Whatever it was they were on about, this was clearly **"big people business"** that Mum didn't want **the Twinzies** or me to know about. Maybe they were going to tell us at some point about a certificate that Grandad had achieved or another prize that he'd won? I kept quiet as I didn't want to spoil their surprise.

Just then, Mrs Turner appeared. Mrs Turner has a knack of turning up whenever something's brewing. I swear there's a trapdoor somewhere in my house that she pops in and out of without anyone noticing. Mrs Turner is always immaculately dressed when she comes over. Her brown hair is usually set in stiff curls, like she's ironed it with curlers still in. She wears a bit of pink lipstick, painted carefully onto her pinched lips, with a round dollop of blusher splodged onto each cheek to liven up her pale white skin.

"Hello, Sharon," she simpered. "It's been a while. Still dressing to…hmm…impress, I see."

"You all right, Mrs T?" Auntie Sharon replied. "Still

keeping yourself going by poking around in other people's business, I see."

The air was colder than the ice cream we'd had for pudding the day before. And Dad choked on the cup of coffee he was drinking.

"Touché, Sha!" I heard Dad splutter.

This head-to-head didn't put Mrs Turner off — she sat down next to Dad on the sofa, wriggling her bottom like a bird sitting down on its freshly laid eggs, in it for the long haul.

Auntie Sharon seamlessly resumed her conversation with Mum and Grandad. "Anyway, Daddy, I just want to make sure you're okay. You look a bit thin and you're getting dark circles under your eyes." She gurned at Mum. "We have to make sure we're looking after Daddy, Cheryl."

Mum sucked her cheeks in a bit more, so much so that I thought her face was going to disappear into itself.

That's when Dad knew he had to step in.

"So, Sharon, how's tricks? How's that boyfriend of yours? What's his name again? Mikel? Michael?"

"Who, Mitch?" Auntie Sharon exclaimed suddenly and

very loudly. "Puh! That wattless light bulb! I ditched him long time ago, man. You have to get rid of things that are bad for your health. **You listen to your Auntie Sha, Sunshine. Don't forget to keep the receipt.**" Then she tapped her nose again in a very knowing way. But I had no idea what she was on about.

That's another good thing about Auntie Sharon, "she's a fascinating mystery". Grampie Clive called her that once and Mrs Turner overheard and said, "You're right. Just like Bigfoot."

It was at this point that Auntie Sharon fully took my presence in.

"Cheryl, what in the sweet baby Jesus's name did you do to this poor child's head?" Auntie Sharon shouted as she bent over and started fiddling with my hair.

I swear I saw Mum roll her sleeves up at that point. Dad swept in to save the day, but **the Twinzies** beat him to it. Auntie Sharon's knickers must have been showing over the waistband of her jeans as she bent over.

"Auntie Sha-Sha's pants are red and frilly!" Lena Twinzie shouted at the top of her voice.

"And they look much smaller than your pants, Mummy. Your pants are massive!" chimed Peter.

Grandad Bobby boomed with laughter. Mum's face turned as red as Auntie Sharon's pants. Mrs Turner asked for a strong cup of tea.

"Why don't you help Sunshine with some ideas for her assembly?" Dad said to Auntie Sharon fifteen minutes later, once everyone had had a chance to recover.

Auntie Sharon sprang to life, jumping like a boxer into the centre of the ring — otherwise known as the living-room rug. "Right! **First things first — hit me with your hit list, Sunny.** What have you got in mind? I'm good at thinking outside of any boxes."

I ran through the ideas from my original list one by one, except the one about the gardening demonstration and Rose Pepper, to avoid upsetting Mum.

"Not bad, not bad," said Auntie Sharon thoughtfully, as she paced across the living room like Sherlock Holmes, but in heels and without the famous hat. "You just need to add some spice here and there. Gymnastics... Yes, I see your problem. You don't want to send anyone flying into the audience again. Any good on a pogo stick or a unicycle?"

I shook my head. Everyone looked baffled. How would this help? Those activities sounded more dangerous than the gymnastics. And I didn't appreciate the reminder about when I knocked Marcus "Donkey" Cruickshank off the stage at the school nativity.

"Pity. A pogo stick or a unicycle would demonstrate your athletic ability, but you could just jump up and down or roll backwards and forwards on the spot. Less carnage."

That explanation didn't help the bafflement.

"Hmm, I have a few outfits that I've shimmied across the Caribbean in. You could borrow them and do a Caribbean-queen fashion show to demonstrate your love of geography," continued Auntie Sharon.

"NO! Next!" shouted Mum.

Mrs Turner asked for another cup of tea.

"Okay, well there's the pizza party idea… Chuck in a couple of bottles of red wine and do it Italian stylee, and you might be on to something. Or a pina colada cocktail! That's got pineapple in it, like a Hawaiian pizza. Ooh, yes, I doubt the teachers would say no."

Mum's mouth shot open, but she didn't get the chance to speak.

"Well, thank you, Auntie Sharon, for those illuminating visions," said Dad, closing down the discussion rather abruptly. "Speaking of food, **dinner's ready. Let's eat!**"

Auntie Sharon's ideas weren't so much thinking outside of any boxes, they were more or less thinking outside of this universe. Full marks for effort though.

Grandad didn't join us for dinner — instead he went up to his room for a lie-down, but not before he'd slipped a rolled-up wedge of papers that looked like they had the Queen's head on them into the pocket of Dariuszkz's tracksuit top.

Grandad winked at me before he went up to his room and said, "Nah worry, we'll think of something for the assembly."

I watched Grandad climb the stairs slowly and carefully, holding on to the banister as he went. Usually, **the Twinzies** and me would be racing him up them. But not on that day. Grandad was tired. And it didn't seem the right time to ask him about the test he'd taken or what prize he might have won.

Two hours later, Auntie Sharon and Dariuszkz had gone. She left in a taxi, of course. Just like in a soap opera.

"Let me know if you need any more ideas or help with practising for your assembly. I was born for the stage," shouted Auntie Sharon very dramatically as the taxi drove away.

"You can say that again," muttered Mum.

"AND WE'LL WORK ON THE HAIR – DON'T WORRY!" she cried as the taxi disappeared into the distance.

I wished Auntie Sharon *was* destined for the stage – because then she could have taken my place on it.

And I still didn't have one decent idea for the assembly.

13

JE M'APPELLE SUNSHINE

On Monday, Miss Peach set us an English writing task to be completed in class that day. I wasn't really in the mood for it, to be honest. Even though Miss Peach's infectious energy could usually win anyone around, I felt tired. I hadn't slept very well over the weekend. My sleep had been overtaken by bad dreams.

On Saturday night, **I'd dreamed that I was in a lifeboat in the middle of the sea – and Grandad was in the water.** He reached out to grab my hand and then a sudden, gusting wind carried the lifeboat away and all I could see through the mist was Grandad's hand waving desperately from an untouchable distance, and I couldn't get back to him.

And then on Sunday night, following Auntie Sharon's visit, I'd had another dream. I was standing in the middle of an empty stage, with a full spotlight beaming straight at me. I felt confident. Happy. But then I opened my mouth and started chanting "Donkey" over and over again, and careered off the stage on a unicycle. My classmates' parents' faces then appeared, whirring in and out like they were in the middle of a kaleidoscope. **And they all started pointing and laughing at me.**

But maybe there was something, some gold dust for the assembly that I could sift from all the nonsense in my dreams. Auntie Sharon's ideas had at least got me thinking. And I'd been trying to work on an idea that had suddenly come to me when I'd woken from one of my dreams. Maybe, just maybe...

But now, here I was, sitting in class, about to make one of the biggest mistakes of my life.

Miss Peach cleared her throat to quieten the class down. "When I was at school, my young fledglings, I had a pen pal."

There were groans around the room.

"Wait a minute! Wait a minute!" she continued. "My pen pal Marie-Claire Binoche is now a teacher at a school in France and teaches a class of children your age. Our paths have virtually mirrored each other, and we both thought it would be a great idea if we carried out an **exchange of our cultures**."

We began to get excited. Were we going to France?

"And what better way to learn about a country if we can't get to visit it" — more groans — "than to **share ideas by writing to each other!**" Miss Peach clapped her hands together in delight. "I have a list of pupils at Miss Binoche's school and I've allocated you all someone to write to, so you can tell them about yourselves, your lives and your interests. You will write first and then your pen pals will write back to you. Any questions?"

Marcus Cruickshank's hand flew up. Marcus's arm must be attached to an electric pulley which automatically swings into action whenever a teacher asks, "Are there any questions?" I wouldn't mind but, even though I like Marcus, sometimes he can ask really silly questions. A bit like **the Twinzies** do — but they're six and he's not.

"So do we have to write to them in French then, Miss?" asked Marcus.

"Good question, Marcus," chirped Miss Peach.

Oh.

Marcus flashed a look around the class as if to say, *You see, look who doesn't ask dumb questions after all!*

"No, Marcus, we will write to them in English, as this is an English writing lesson. The children are very keen to learn and to practise their grasp of the language, so they will also write back to us in English."

"So it's a win-win for us then!" blurted Marcus.

"Hmm," said Miss Peach. "I wouldn't quite put it that way. I would say it's…it's mutual support. You get to learn how to write a good letter as well as learn about French culture, and they get to learn about you and hone their English grammatical skills. Has anyone here been to France?"

Barely a second had passed before Evie put her hand up. She was starting to give Marcus a run for his money.

Evie told us she'd been to Paris for the weekend with her parents and sister a few years ago, and that they'd visited places called the **Arc de Triomphe** and the **Louvre Museum**, which I'd never heard of, but she'd also been to the **Eiffel Tower** — one of the most famous attractions in the whole, entire world! The only thing missing from her story was the actor **George Rooney** turning up in his posh sports car and giving her a piggyback to the top of the tower. Oof!

Once Evie had told her tale and Miss Peach had calmed down from the excitement (because she'd been to all of those tourist attractions too) we were given the names of our pen pals and a run-through of how to structure our letters.

My pen pal is called Elise Baptiste. I like her name — it's rhymey and sing-songy.

"You are allowed to write anything you want — *within reason*," said Miss Peach firmly.

This assignment should have been right up my street, because I love English. I gave it quite a bit of thought, desperately trying to come up with something to write that was interesting enough to impress Elise. It was only when I looked around and noticed Evie taking a sneak peek across at me that I bolted into action.

I told Elise about Grandad Bobby, because most of the rest of my family aren't that interesting. I wrote about Charley and Arun, and **I couldn't help but mention Evie Evans. Evie this. Evie that. Evie, you're so brilliant.** That was all I ever heard these days and **it was really getting on my nerves**.

I started to get into the swing of things, feeling good about getting a lot off my chest and onto the page. Letter writing was turning out to be a great project.

Then I paused, pencil at my lips, looking over what I'd written. On reflection, I hadn't been the kindest to Evie in the words I'd used — **a pain, irritating and annoying** all made her sound like some terrible body ailment rather than the person at school who I'd been hand-picked to look after. Sure she got on my nerves, but...

I put my hand up to ask Miss Peach for a fresh piece of paper to have another go at the letter.

It was too late.

"Time's up!" Miss Peach trilled.

"But—" I said hopelessly.

"No buts, you've all had plenty of time to offer a flavour of yourselves," said Miss Peach.

But what if the flavour of yourself you'd offered was more sour than a cupful of vinegar?

"Please place your letters in the envelopes provided and seal them, adding the name of your pen pal onto the front of the envelope, and copying the address that is on the board," said Miss Peach.

I gulped down my sourness, realizing it was too late to scribble anything out.

"Are you okay, Sunshine?" asked Miss Peach, when I handed the letter in. **"You look a little flushed."**

"Yes, Miss Peach, I'm fine." I was lying because I knew that if Evie or Miss Peach ever found out what was written in that letter, I wouldn't be fine, I'd be very un-fine indeed. Thank goodness no one would ever know.

"Oh, just one more thing," said Miss Peach at the end of the lesson. "So we can mix up the communication styles, we'll be broadcasting the jubilee assembly live to Miss

Binoche's class in France, via Zoom, so they can see us in action. Isn't that amazing? You'll be just like **film stars**."

That wasn't amazing at all — I didn't want to be a film star. The thought of walking out onto the school stage was bad enough, but now we'd be zoomed live to France as well? Was there no end to the stresses of **school-dom**? At least there was one good thing about this new disaster — it stopped me from panicking over the letter I'd written to Elise Baptiste. For now.

14

GOING VIRAL

The playground was alive with the sound of very excited schoolchildren at lunchtime. Now that the stakes had been elevated, everyone, unsurprisingly, wanted to shine.

"So what happens now that the jubilee assembly's turned into a nuclear bomb?" Arun asked Charley and me, using his hands to expertly demonstrate his brain exploding out of the top of his head.

I couldn't have put it better myself. There was no stopping this thing from **GOING VIRAL!** It was bad enough worrying about how I was going to impress Miss Peach, but now I would have to find something to impress a national and international audience.

"Well, I'm stuffed," said Arun.

"Why are you stuffed when we haven't had lunch yet?" I asked absent-mindedly. Come on! I was completely distracted, mainly due to wallowing in my own misery.

Arun and Charley looked at each other with raised eyebrows and then simultaneously gave me a sympathetic pat on the back.

"I meant, I have no ideas at all," said Arun.

"Are you kidding me? You have the world at your very fingertips." I wriggled my fingers to emphasize the point. "You are so talented, Arun."

"Really?" asked Arun, not seeming quite as sure.

I nodded enthusiastically, trying to eliminate any of his doubt.

"I've got it!" I declared loudly, trying to whip up Arun's excitement levels, which actually made him and Charley jump a few centimetres into the air. "**You're a fantastic singer and dancer.** And you know loads about Hollywood musicals and Bollywood films. You are brilliantly creative, Arun. Why don't you do something that combines the two?"

"Yes, well no one really knows about my thing for musicals or singing or dancing except for you two and my parents. It's a secret," said Arun, sounding more than a little defensive.

Erm, I was pretty sure Arun's love of musicals was the worst kept secret in town. He'd never realized, but there were telltale signs. Like the time on his seventh birthday when we played pass the parcel to the soundtrack of **The Greatest Showman**. Or walking down the street with him he might suddenly do a high kick, spin, two-step or slide — and if he's being really fancy, he'll break into a moonwalk.

"Well, Arun, let your secret be a secret no more," I said gently. **"Don't hide your light under a bush – or something like that."**

Arun began blowing air furiously out of his top lip at his fringe, as if he was telling it off. Then, suddenly, he beamed a film-star smile at Charley and me. "Yes — maybe I could do an **East-meets-West Bolly/Hollywood** dual fusion of the influences."

"Erm…yes, okay, Arun. Sounds great!" I had no idea

what he was talking about. But if it was coming from Arun, I knew it would be practised to perfection.

"What about you, Charley, should we help you with an idea?" I asked.

"That's okay. I know what I'm doing, and I have my costume sorted out already," chirped Charley.

"Spill the beans!" I said.

"Yes, tell all!" said Arun.

"I'm going to do some Irish dancing. I'll use my outfit from when I performed in the St Patrick's Day Parade. I just hope I remember all the steps," said Charley.

"That's a genius idea, Charley!" I said excitedly.

"It's perfect!" said Arun.

Charley grinned. The St Patrick's Day Parade is really important to Charley's family — they take part in it every year. St Patrick is the patron saint of Ireland and big celebrations are held each March, with parades, music and dancing — and everyone wears green. Well, that's what Charley says anyway.

Charley and Arun were both beaming now. We high-fived each other and then danced around in a circle, weaving in and out, linking and unlinking arms and woo-hooing in a dance that would have seen Grandad Bobby clapping for joy.

We were so engrossed that we didn't notice Evie come up behind us. She had Maya Watkins and Izzy James in tow. Maya, Izzy and Evie were hanging out together a lot now. I suppose a bit like Arun, Charley and me. What could I say? I was glad she was happy.

"What are you doing?" asked Evie.

"Nothing. Just coming up with ideas for the jubilee assembly," I replied.

"Tell me, tell me!" said Evie, jumping to her tiptoes and clapping her hands in excitement.

Hmph! Maybe Evie should have been so excited when I'd asked her to share **her** ideas with **me**.

Arun and Charley 'fessed up what they were going to do. I was happy for my friends, but I still wasn't one hundred per cent sold on the idea I'd had for myself — and I was too embarrassed to test it out there and then.

"Well, since you're both going to dance, Arun and Charley, I might sing. I can do either. My mum says I was born to sing and dance," Evie said proudly. Maya and Izzy nodded approvingly.

My face didn't move to give away my feelings, but in my mind my eyeballs were rolling backwards and forwards like marbles.

To be fair, Evie is a great singer. Sometimes she'd start singing in the playground at break and lunch, if there was a new song she liked in the charts. Once, when I'd started singing along with her, she'd told me that my voice was really deep: "Haha! **You sound like you've swallowed a wheelbarrow-load of gravel.** But don't worry, people with the deepest voices are often the best singers."

She must have noticed that I'd looked down in my horsey mouth about that, because then she tried to cheer me up, by making up a song on the spot about having a deep voice.

It went something like this:

"Her voice is deep,

But she's very sweet.

It's not a blow,

But Sunny's voice is very, very LOW."

She sang that last bit like she was playing the deepest, lowest note on a trombone. Which reminded me to ask my parents to add throat lozenges to the weekly shopping list.

"I hope I haven't upset you, Sunny," she'd said at the time. "My sister says I talk too much and that I'm a bit of a know-it-all."

I'd shaken my head.

"You will tell me if I say anything to upset you, won't you, Sunny?"

I'd nodded.

That was two fibs told in less than a minute. But how could I upset the new girl by telling her the truth? I figured that if I just let her keep talking, she might eventually…stop?

But now, months later, here we were and Evie was still talking.

"What about you, Sunny? What are you going to do at the assembly?" Evie asked.

My skin started to prickle with heat. I scratched at my forehead and neck, and my feet developed a nervous twitch, making me do an awkward shuffly dance from foot to foot.

"Why don't you sing one of Grandad Bobby's songs?" said Charley, sensing that all was not well.

"Hmm…that sounds okay. And I'm sure Sunny will be able to sing really well because of her gravelly voice. But if she thinks hard enough, I'm sure there's something more interesting she can do," said Evie, back in her teacher mode. "But whatever you do, **don't fall over onstage again, Sunny**. I loved it when you told me about tripping up during the nativity but you don't want it to be a habit. It's those long legs! **Silly Sunny!**" Evie smiled to herself at a memory that didn't belong to her.

I only had myself to blame. I did tell Evie that story. It was a way to help her settle in when she first started school. I wanted to make her laugh, so she didn't feel as nervous. Now the joke was very much on me.

But Evie was right. I needed something more interesting for myself. Everyone had heard Grandad's songs before, and they were more about Grandad and his personality than about me. I wanted something new, something fresh and exciting. The pizza-making, gymnastics, countries that I want to visit, times tables and gardening didn't make the cut — but what if I could spin the ideas into something different? What's more, I was starting to feel increasing pressure after Charley and Arun had decided what they were doing. It was time to be brave and get on with it.

"I can help you, if you like," said Evie. "You can come over to my house and we can bake cakes for brain food and come up with a plan."

I shook my head firmly. **"No thanks, Evie. I've got this."**

Evie's face fell into a frown.

"Sometimes the old things are the best things. My mum always says, **'Work with what you've got'**," said Charley.

I smiled, grateful for Charley's backing. I just wasn't so sure I had anything to work with. And time was running out. The assembly was in July and it was now the middle of May. It still seemed a long way off, but Miss Peach couldn't be stalled for much longer. She was keen to hear all our ideas so that she could give them the all-clear, and we could start practising straight after half-term.

But would my idea be good enough? My body tingled with the thought.

15

SOUR STRAWBERRY

I wasn't ready to talk about my idea for the assembly in the playground. I knew it needed work. Major surgery. But at least I had the bones of something. It just needed fleshing out.

Charley's mum, Maria, picked us up from school that day. Mum and Dad were going to take it in turns to finish work a bit earlier, as *they* had decided that Grandad wouldn't be looking after us for a while. No one had asked me or **the Twinzies** whether we were okay with this new arrangement, I might add. But, anyway, today Maria was dropping us home for some reason. And Mum had invited them to stay for tea.

Maybe we were all going to present Grandad with his certificate that everyone had been so **hush–hush** about when Auntie Sharon had been round, I thought.

But anyway, Charley and I were going to make the most of the opportunity of being over at mine and think of ideas for the assembly. And maybe, just maybe, I might show her what I had in mind. And Grandad too!

Charley's mum might have picked us up, but I knew Mum would still have made sure she got home a little earlier to start frantically cleaning — even though we'd done that at the weekend already. Whenever anyone comes over, Mum goes into a tailspin, tidying, bleaching and polishing. She even polished Dad's head once, mistaking him for an ornament.

Not that our house is some kind of dump, you understand — she just likes it to look like one of those pristine places she's always watching on the telly.

Dad doesn't like Mum watching shows about other people's houses because he thinks it gives her "fanciful ideas about escaping to the country". He says that Mum screams whenever she sees a spider in the bath, so he doesn't know how she'd cope with them running all over the place if she moved somewhere where there's more grass than concrete.

Basically, if Mum could clear us three kids away to make the house look extra tidy, I'm sure she would, but I don't like to fill her head with those kinds of ideas.

Anyway, I'm getting distracted again.

I was very excited that Charley was coming over. And now that she had revealed her plans, she'd promised to practise her dance in front of me too. But I was still fretting about my idea.

"I don't know what's got into you lately, Sunshine. You're usually so positive. We'll think of something," said Charley on our way to my house.

I didn't know what had got into me either. And Evie was starting to get under my skin again. **Look at me, I sing and dance. I can do both brilliantly. I'm more brilliant than the brilliantest person in the whole, wide world. Oof!** Never mind about the school's fiftieth anniversary celebrations, I was convinced it would take me another fifty years to recover from all the boasting and bragging.

To be honest, it would have been nice to go over to Charley's, in the hope that a change of scenery would inspire me, but Charley's house is always so busy.

Charley has four big sisters. Her family reminds me of a set of Russian dolls because they look so alike — rosy cheeks, reddish-blonde hair, big blue eyes, dinky noses — but each sister is slightly older and bigger than the next, and their mum is number-one doll! Their hair gets bigger as well. From Charley's straight, neat bob, by the time you get up to her eldest sister, Shannon, her hair is about a metre wide and glued together with lots of hairspray and hairpins to keep it in place. She also smells like the inside of a hairdresser's salon. Charley's mum has the biggest hair of all: waves of natural curls close in on her round face, like she's a yeti — though a very pretty-looking yeti, I must say.

"Keep up, you two," shouted Charley's mum, as she walked along holding **the Twinzies**' hands. She didn't really shout. It was like if an angel shouted — like a heavenly chorus. She's really kind, Charley's mum. She has to be, because she's a nurse. **"And please pick up your bags off the floor. They aren't suitcases with wheels."**

"Yes, Maria. I mean, yes, Charley's mum!" I shouted absent-mindedly, not really listening and still dragging my school bag along the pavement.

Charley and I kept a reasonable distance away. I wanted to talk to her about something without any other listening ears.

"Erm, Charley, Evie's really something else, isn't she?"

Charley's eyes widened. **"You mean she's an alien from outer space?** I knew it!"

"Erm, well, no. I wasn't thinking extraterrestrial. I meant whoa! Woo-hoo! She's, like, **wow!**" I threw my arms out, flailing them about in the air to demonstrate.

Charley thought for a few seconds, unfazed by my random hand gestures. "Actually, **I think she has a head as big as a watermelon**. She's a lot of a show-off. It's hard though, isn't it? Because she's the newest girl in our class, and everyone likes her, you want her to feel a part of things. And you don't want to come across like you're being a sour strawberry by saying anything. Maybe it's **new-girl nerves**? Maybe? But then Daisy Sanders was new in Year

Four and she's not like Evie at all. I doubt anybody is."

Oh. I hadn't expected such a detailed answer. But **exactly**. New-girl nerves, that's what Mum had said. I couldn't say Evie was overconfident, because Grandad always said it's good to have confidence in your own abilities. And I didn't want to say she was being mean, because Evie always said everything with such a radiant smile, with no nastiness in her voice. And I hadn't wanted to tell her she was getting on my nerves, because...because I didn't want to come across like **a sour strawberry**.

Before I had a chance to say anything further, we had arrived at our doorstep. I waved at Mrs Turner, who was on patrol at her front gate across the road.

"You should get her some binoculars," said Charley.

I nodded in agreement.

16

THE AROSA STAR

As expected, the house was so shiny I could have put skates on and ice-danced across it.

Mum ushered us all into the kitchen and put the kettle on. What is it about grown-ups that they always feel the need to boil water and make bitter cups of tea and coffee? When I'm older, I'll put the milk on and make loads of cups of hot chocolate with humongous amounts of cream, marshmallows and chocolate sprinkles on top.

Mum and Charley's mum huddled together whispering by the kitchen sink. Honestly, when grown-ups do their secretive **"big-people talking"** it's fine — but when us kids start speaking quietly, they immediately think we're up to something. **So unfair**.

"Is who mi can hear chatting 'bout me?" said Grandad as he made a grand entrance into the kitchen. "Ahh, it's you, Charley, and you've brought Mum too? Well, what an honour." Grandad, though he hadn't been his usual self for a while, still sidled up to Charley's mum, took her hand gently and kissed it like some smoothie-chops from an old movie.

"Oh, Dad!" said Mum, looking totally embarrassed.

"Is wha mi do now?" said Grandad, like butter wouldn't melt in his mouth. And then, as if he'd been zapped with a laser beam of new energy, he went into one of his stage acts.

"We must cook something special for dinner, Cheryl. Is why you never tell me before we were having such salubrious guests? Tell me, Charley and Charley's mum, you want some **curry goat and rice**?"

As delicious as that dish is, I was getting a bit embarrassed myself now. But Grandad had started to enjoy himself, so there was no stopping him.

"Some **cow foot or oxtail and butter beans?**"

"**Ugh!** Grandad!"

Charley's face looked like she'd been asked to eat Bambi, but her mum wasn't put off. She laughed. "I think rustling up those delicious delicacies would take a bit longer than we've got, but I wouldn't say no to a slice of **bun and cheese**." Charley's mum winked at Grandad, and then I could have sworn I saw one or two tears forming in her eyes.

I didn't think it was that funny, but Grandad roared with laughter. "**Heh-hey — what a ting! You hear dat, Cheryl? She knows more about Caribbean food than you two Simpsons right here in this room.**"

"Yes, thank you, Daddy," said Mum, putting one hand on her waist and pursing her lips. "Charley and Sunshine are going to discuss ideas for the school's jubilee assembly. Why don't you help them come up with something as creative as your ideas for our evening meal?" Then Mum turned to Charley and reassured her quietly, "And how about some spaghetti bolognese for tea?"

Charley smiled a Cheshire Cat grin — she loves spaghetti bolognese.

Mum and Charley's mum left us to it, nattering while Mum cooked. And Charley, Grandad Bobby and me all sat around the kitchen table.

Grandad drew in his chair closer to the table, leaned in and smiled. **"Now the old folks are out of the way, let's get creative,"** he said.

Charley and I giggled, instantly relaxing into the task at hand. We told Grandad about how we'd now have to perform our pieces in front of our French pen pals.

"*Oui, oui, mon ami.* The stakes are high — whewie! What you got, Miss Chaar-ley?" said Grandad with a flourish.

Charley talked through her Irish dance routine and told Grandad all about the St Patrick's Day Parade she'd performed at in March. She'd even got to travel through the streets on a float covered in Irish flags, four-leaf clovers and a giant, green leprechaun's hat. "They're for luck." Charley grinned.

"Wear green and you'll definitely be seen." Grandad smiled. **"It's a great thing to be proud of where you're from,** Charley."

Charley's beam grew wider. Even though I tried to fight my feelings, I was starting to feel a little bit green myself — with envy. Not about Charley dancing at the show. Not that. She had come up with something that really meant something to her, which was the whole point of **Why X is important to me**. But it was like everyone else's ideas were so much more exciting and had more meaning than what I had come up with.

I was starting to feel wobbly about sharing my idea with Charley and Grandad. I had intended to surprise them, but now I wasn't so sure. Auntie Sharon had said to **"add some spice"**, so I'd started to write something, stringing together all the ideas from my original list. But would it be enough to wow everyone?

"So now that you have everything just so, Charley, what about little Miss Sunshine? Still want to do some gardening?" asked Grandad, interrupting my thoughts.

I shrugged.

"Well, the weather's really brightened up out there, why don't we join **the Twinzies** in the garden? It might spark some ideas and you'll have some room to show me your dance, Charley," said Grandad.

Charley jumped out of her chair at the prospect. My chair screeched along the kitchen floor tiles, like Grandad had announced he was about to drag me through a field of stinging nettles without any shoes or socks on.

But I was so glad we did end up outside. I'd been so preoccupied with thoughts about the Golden Jubilee assembly, and about Evie, that **I hadn't noticed what a beautiful day it had turned out to be**. In the morning it had rained that kind of thin, almost invisible rain that looks like spaghetti; it sneaks up on you, so you end up getting drenched before you even notice what's happening. Luckily (yeah, whatever) Mum always makes us carry a light, unfashionable raincoat in our bags whatever the season, so I'd stayed pretty dry. But now I had to raise my hands to shield my eyes from the bold brightness that had broken through. The grey, moody day had come to life, like the sun was winking at us saying, *You see, I'm not just glorious at the height of summer, you know. I can outshine myself on any day of the year!*

I glanced over at Grandad. He was looking up towards

the sun too, with his eyes closed. His smile increased slowly as the rays gently tickled his face.

"Is Jamaica as hot as this?" asked Charley.

"Of course it is, Charley," I huffed. "It's in the Caribbean!"

Charley's face crumpled. I felt bad.

Grandad opened his eyes and sat down on one of the garden chairs. "Yes, Jamaica is hotter, but the sunlight reminds me of my first day in this country, when **I stepped off that ship** after being closed up for three whole weeks. We'd sailed straight through, without any stops — but the sun shone brightly to welcome us when we arrived."

"Three weeks!" Charley exclaimed, pulling up a seat next to Grandad. "Why didn't **you just get on a plane** and get here in a zap!"

"Aha! Well, in those days it was easier and cheaper to travel by ship," said Grandad, inhaling deeply like he was lifting the memories from somewhere deep within his body. "The ships sailed more often than the planes flew. Many people know about the **Windrush**, but there were more ships. **I came on the Arosa Star**. Bwoy, she was mighty and strong."

"What did you do for three whole weeks in the middle of the ocean? I'd be so bored," asked Charley.

"Well, it wasn't so bad," said Grandad. "We played games on deck, sang, danced, had a tot or two of rum, that kind of thing. But when the wind blew and we got caught in a storm — whew! Then there was trouble! The **Arosa Star** stayed firm, but all on deck would blow away: tables, chairs, us. All the furniture had to be strapped down. We just had to go and sit in our cabins until the heavens decided to settle."

"I'm glad it didn't rain on your first day here after travelling all that way, that would have been horrible," said Charley.

Grandad looked towards us both and his eyes twinkled. "Yes, it was **as glorious a day as I've ever seen: full of hope**. And then the next day it rained, and then it rained the day after that, and the day after that. But God had a plan. If I'd have known how soggy this land can be, I would have picked up my suitcase, turned back onto that ship and spent another three weeks going home again!" We all chuckled.

"But I don't understand, why would you come here in the first place, Grandad Bobby? Jamaica looks so happy and yellow and green on the telly," continued Charley.

Grandad considered this for a moment. "**Jamaica is beautiful.** It's even better when you see it with your own eyes and touch it with your own hands. Bwoy! You're right, Charley, **the green trees, the yellow sands, the blue waters, the white rum. Heh-hey!** All these wonders are truly a sight to behold." Grandad's eyes shone brightly. "**But this country has many good points too.** And don't forget, young Charley, the land of your ancestors, Ireland, isn't called the Emerald Isle for nothing. It's very beautiful too."

Charley nodded knowingly.

"So, like what, Grandad? What are the good things about being here? I still don't understand why you would leave your home and your family," I asked.

"There was an **invitation from the British government** to help rebuild the country after the Second World War. Many came to answer the call from '**the mother country**'. Some came for the **opportunities, work, further education**, that sort of thing. I wanted to earn more **money to send home** to help my parents and my brothers and sisters with our farm. Maybe I thought I would find that pot of gold at the end of the rainbow, or streets paved with gold — that's what many of us thought. But the reality didn't always live up to the dream. **Getting used to a new way of life, leaving all I'd known behind, was hard.** Yes, there were some people who didn't like us coming here and didn't make us feel welcome. For some of us, it was difficult to find housing or jobs. But I also met some very nice people along the way. It was an adventure. You know I like adventure — and without being here, I wouldn't have you all."

160

"Don't you miss your home, Grandad? Don't you miss Jamaica?" I asked.

"I do. Yes, I do. **But I also believe that home is where your heart is and that's right here with you.** But do you know what I do if I ever miss back home in Jamaica?"

Grandad waited for my answer. I shrugged. "I don't know, Grandad — cry?"

He smiled. "No, I always look up and see the stars. **Wherever you are in this world, look up and see the stars and you know you are never far away from home.** You see that big map you have on the wall in your bedroom? It's the world — make it come to life. One day, go and see it all and have your own adventures. Life is always an adventure, never forget that."

Even though I do love geography and languages and other countries, I'm always paying attention to everyone else's stories and I'd never really thought about our own story and Jamaica so deeply before. Yes, we do very Jamaican things and follow traditions like having **bun and**

cheese and **fried fish on Good Friday**, going to church on Easter Sunday, eating **rice and peas** — one of our traditional Jamaican dishes — most Sundays, and having delicious **fried plantains** as a treat for weekend breakfasts. But I was so used to those things, they hadn't seemed special. I suppose you don't appreciate things as much when it's happening on your own doorstep every day.

Jamaica always seemed so near, but yet so far. And now, hearing Grandad speak in that way with Charley and me, it sounded like a land of beauty and wonder. Grandad was a real adventurer. After all, he'd been back to Jamaica to live with Grandma Pepper and Mum and Auntie Sharon. I knew he'd even been to America. I wondered whether the same energy and passion for life ran through my bones.

"You're so brave, Grandad. I'm so glad that you're my grandad," I said.

"Woo, where did that dust come from?" said Grandad, wiping at his eyes. "Come, enough about me. I want to know, any more ideas for the golden day?"

I shrugged. Shrugging had become my new favourite thing. It was a shame I couldn't choose it as an option for the assembly. I'd have been quite happy having a shrug-off with myself. "It's just a boring old assembly, Grandad," I said.

"I think Sunny should sing one of your songs," chirped Charley, probably trying to be helpful.

It wasn't helpful at all in my mind. I'd been thinking about what Evie had said about Grandad's songs and poems — that everyone had heard them all before. More than anything else, I wanted to be exciting — definitely **not** old Silly Sunny. And now Charley, and even Grandad, were getting in my way, trying to force Grandad's songs on me.

Grandad's face shone. "What do you think, Sunshine?"

I softened. I didn't want to disappoint Grandad, but I also wanted to do my own thing.

"I don't know, Grandad, I've been kind of thinking about another idea."

Grandad didn't deliberately show it, but I thought I saw a hint of a shadow cast across his face — or maybe it was because the sun had just gone in. He smiled. "I'm pleased for you, my sweet Sunshine."

"About time!" shouted Peter Twinzie from across the lawn.

"Show us then," said Lena.

The Twinzies had stopped chasing each other around the garden to listen in on the conversation.

The Twinzies, Charley and even Grandad all looked at me expectantly for the big reveal.

Could I do this? I just had to conjure up some of Auntie Sharon's energy. She may have had some wacky thoughts on what I could do at the assembly, but she had still worked with my original ideas. I wouldn't be shimmying across the stage in one of Auntie Sharon's outfits to demonstrate my love of geography, or using a pogo stick or a unicycle to show off my athletic skills, but maybe, just maybe, I could work in a different, more subtle way by combining all the things I love into an awe-inspiring poem. That was it! That was my plan. And that's what I'd been working on.

In my head, within the comfort and safety of the four walls of my bedroom, it had seemed brilliant. But now, standing in front of the people who knew me so well, it felt like I was about to go rock climbing without any ropes.

"Well, Charley and I are both going to practise, so she goes first," I said firmly, but admittedly, I might have been a bit chicken. She owed me one though, for saying that to Grandad about me singing one of his songs.

"No, you go first…" said Charley.

I clearly hadn't been firm enough. "No! You go first…"

Charley and I had a debate for a few seconds, before Peter Twinzie stepped in.

"Toot…toot…toot…toot…toot!"

Peter turned his fists into a trumpet and declared by fanfare, "Ladies and gentlemen! Children and Grandad! We now present the performances we've all been waiting for… *FOR E-VER*! **First to perform is the SUPERFROGGY-CRAGGYLISTICALLY AWESOME Charley!"**

Charley looked like a rabbit caught in very bright headlights. She bravely accepted her fate, shrugged and got on with it.

She stretched her legs a little and began jigging to an invisible beat that lived somewhere in her head, using our decking as a stage. Grandad and **the Twinzies** started to clap in time with her. Nimbly, effortlessly, elegantly, she performed like a true pro.

"Whoop, whoop, whoop!" the Twinzies shrieked in excitement.

Grandad then started beatboxing, using his mouth to make sounds like a drum, to accompany the dancing. It sounded more like the theme tune to *Blue Peter* than an Irish jig, to be honest, but it seemed to spur Charley on. She climbed higher and higher into the air with her kicks. The noise was so raucous that it drew Mum and Charley's mum into the garden. They cheered and clapped along too.

Charley bowed at the end of her performance and was met with rapturous applause. Charley was **fantastic**! I beamed and gave her a high five.

It was my turn. Silence fell. They were waiting. My fingers, face, even my toes felt like they were sweating, despite the increasing chilliness in the air as evening drew closer. An empty white sheet of paper spread out across my mind.

"It's okay, Sunny, take your time," said Mum, her voice echoing into the silence.

"Erm...erm...I'm, I'm going to recite a poem about...

no, no I don't know…" The more I thought about it, the more I realized what a silly idea my stupid poem was. And no, I am not being hard on myself. Seriously, these were the first two lines of my first attempt at the poem:

Pizza is my sister,
It's better than getting a blister.

And I was supposed to be good at English!

I opened my mouth. Nothing came out. I lowered my head and put my hand to my throat. **Lost-voice-itis** was striking again. I raised my head slightly and looked across at Grandad, pleading with my eyes for him to help me.

Grandad always helped me — and he didn't miss the silent distress call this time either. But then Grandad went to get up and found it difficult to rise from his seat. Mum and Charley's mum rushed to his side, but he held out his hand to stop them.

"Wait now, wait now!" he told them. "We've taken Sunshine by surprise; she's still working on her act. **Mi will sing something to see us in to dinner.**"

Grandad stayed in his chair and started to sing a song called "**I Can See Clearly Now**" — about the rain going away and it becoming a bright sunshiny day. He sounded a little breathless and raspier than usual, but I figured it was the cool evening air causing the change to his vocals. Anyway, the slight crustiness in his voice didn't matter — the sounds he made were still what I imagine an angel sounds like in heaven.

Later on, in my room, I stared at the small island of Jamaica, floating like a jewel in the Caribbean Sea on my map of the world, and thought about the problem ahead of me. If I dried up like that in front of my own family, then how would I manage in front of all those other people at the jubilee assembly? I wanted to be positive. I wanted to be great! But all I could see stretching ahead of me was failure.

There and then, **I felt like a small island floating alone in the middle of an ocean**.

17

FORGETTING THINGS

For the rest of that week, Arun, Charley and I tried, whenever we could, to make ourselves scarce at breaktimes and lunchtimes. We'd hide just behind the fenced games area, away from nosey eyes (Evie's), but just in view enough so that the teachers wouldn't think we were misbehaving.

Arun showed us a few of his dance moves. Performing in front of us helped him to feel more confident. Charley practised some of her leg kicks and foot taps, as she was worried about getting her steps wrong. With me, we got ever so practical, deciding to be systematic and going through a sensible list of assembly ideas from A-Z.

"**A** — can you pretend you keep an **albatross** in your garden shed?" asked Charley. Arun and I looked at each other and burst out laughing.

"**B — bat keeper**?" said Arun. Riotous laughter from all of us.

This process took a while, and for some reason we kept running with the animal theme. I ended up sounding like the weirdest — or best, depending on how you look at it — zookeeper in history. I mean, the biggest problem with the whole animal alphabet thing was I don't have any pets. **Not a horse, not a dragon, not a dog. Not even a goldfish.** But the game was fun while it lasted, even though I still hadn't settled on anything.

Evie may have spotted us once or twice, but then I'd tugged Charley and Arun away around the fence, to put her off joining us. Evie had Maya and Izzy now, so it didn't matter. It was no skin off my nose that she'd found new best friends. Well, maybe only a little bit of skin.

Even though I'd managed to get a lot of my feelings about her out in the letter to my new French pen pal, Elise Baptiste, I did feel guilty about what I'd written about Evie.

Maybe we could start again, ridding ourselves of this weirdness that had developed between us? But, then again, the whole English Channel separated me from that letter now. So it was probably best to just forget about it. Let Evie do her thing and I'd do mine.

Speaking of weird, **my family was starting to behave very weirdly indeed**. I mean, even weirder than usual. In the week leading up to the half-term break, all the grown-ups were on tender-hooks. I don't know what being on tender-hooks means exactly, but people always say it on TV shows when they're feeling a bit nervous or edgy. Or is it **tenterhooks**? I can never quite hear what they're saying, and I don't know what a tenter is. Anyway, that was what was happening at my house. Everyone was speaking in whispers, talking their **"big people business"** so that **the Twinzies** and I couldn't overhear. Every time I tried to mention **And this is why X is important to me**, Mum smiled vaguely and said, "You'll think of something, Sunny." But I knew she wasn't really listening.

I've always been a good sleeper. As soon as my head hits the pillow, it's usually lights out. You'd have to put a drum kit right next to my bed and play it full whack to try and wake me up. Even then I might whisper "**Nice beat**" at you, roll over and go back to drawing long, deep **zzzzs**. So it was the tossing and turning at night, drifting in and out of sleep after being taunted by bad dreams, that really got to me. I was worrying about being a silly, failing mess, yes — but something else was happening, something I couldn't quite put my finger on.

Dad did try to help me with ideas for the assembly, but it was an unusually half-hearted effort.

"You promised you'd help me, Dad," I said pleadingly. "It's half-term soon and Miss Peach wants us to finalize our ideas and start practising our routines when we get back." I had to make sure Dad was aware of **the ticking time bomb of a deadline** before us. There was a Golden Jubilee assembly lurking in the shadows, ready to eat me. "I keep 'accidentally' dropping my pencil on the floor or excusing myself to go to the loo whenever the word golden starts to fall out of Miss Peach's mouth. By the time she utters 'gold—', I'm gone!" I told him.

Dad tried to refocus, rubbing at his temples with his

fingers as he thought. "Okay, okay. How about we ask the school to get Arthur out of retirement and give him a reboot? He's been a very important part of our lives."

I sighed. "Dad, he was the robot we *(you)* made for my '**engineering of the future**' project two years ago. He was important to *you*, Dad."

"Yes, I suppose he was my first great school creation. I'll never forget him," said Dad, looking off into the distance with cloudy eyes.

Arthur had been fashioned out of bits of old metal, tin cans and cardboard boxes, with his face drawn on, by me, in felt-tip pen. "We need to give him an air of childish simplicity. No one will suspect a thing," Dad had said, muttering to himself as we built, glued and tinkered. And they say children are cunning!

But Dad was right. I got top marks and Arthur has had a starring role at school, standing proudly in reception ever since. He's a little rustier these days, but his painted-on smile is still going strong for all to see. Don't ask me why he's called Arthur. Dad got **the Twinzies** to name him.

"Yes, very regal," said Dad at the time. "I love it!

This could be the start of something great. Just imagine it, a whole new robot range of Arthurs."

The Twinzies beamed. I'd looked doubtful.

"You may mock, Sunshine Simpson, but look at some of the great inventions that Black people have created or helped to improve: traffic light signals, light bulbs, lift doors, gas masks, heart pacemakers, home security systems, lawn mowers, ironing boards, doorknobs and doorstops. Even pencil sharpeners, the ice-cream scoop, crisps and – perhaps most exciting of all – the supersoaker water gun!"

"Whoa! How cool is that?" said **the Twinzies** in unison.

"Precisely," said Dad. **"By this time next year, we could be millionaires."**

Who knows what goes on in my family's brains half the time? And we are still waiting to be millionaires.

Excuse me, I'm getting distracted again…

…And Mum was very distracted as we got to the end of May.

She started to forget things, so everything took twice as long.

Mum forgot her purse when we went to the shops, so we had to double back to get it; she misplaced the car keys; she even put the crisps in the fridge and the milk in the cupboard.

Dad walked around scratching his chin and his head a lot, like he was deep in thought. I would have suspected a case of fleas, but the house is always too clean for any bugs. And Grandad spent most of the time in his room **"lying down"**, **"resting"** or **"taking some time out"**. Grandad always lived life at one hundred miles an hour, but now it seemed like he'd slowed to a crawl. And my dreams, my nightmares, kept haunting me — night after night, I'd wake up feeling terrified.

One of the strangest things of all was Mum introducing takeaways into our lives, because of being so **"out of sorts"**. Mum doesn't usually like takeaway meals, unless it's an occasional convenience food from a local supermarket; she thinks fast food is lazy. She thinks that if you don't simmer things on the hob for decades or bake them in the oven for hours on end then it's not proper cooking.

The trouble was Mum was very stressed because of making meals for everyone and fussing around Grandad. Dad was even going to shuffle his hours around again so he could work from home and help out more. Because, as well as making meals for the rest of us, Mum had started making Grandad lots of green slop, like spinach soup and kale smoothies — anything "**good for the soul**" is a winning recipe in Mum's eyes. She added lots of herbs and spices and muttered to herself things like "**Dad needs extra nutrients**" and "**Turmeric, everyone says add turmeric**". She would stir the pot and liquidize ingredients like she was making a potion.

But it was as if Grandad had been put on a super diet or something, because he was losing even more weight than he had been before and he just didn't look the same any more.

It was bad enough that Grandad had stopped walking us to school, but now he wasn't even going into the garden, so we had to do all the tending of Grandad's plants with Dad. Even Rose Pepper looked a little droopy with the disappointment. Where had my **bodybuilder ox** of a

Grandad gone? Where was **Iron Bobby**? All of me wanted to know and all of me was afraid to ask.

"Let's get something from Burger Palace," said Mum one evening, a couple of days into half-term. I nearly fell off my chair. If we were ever to have takeaways as a treat, that would be at the weekend not on a week night. I thought all my Christmases and New Year's Eve parties had come at once.

"What's at Burger Palace?" asked Peter Twinzie.

"**Burgers**, of course!" I answered without missing a breath. "Let's go!" And I quickly grabbed our coats before Mum could change her mind.

But that night, I found out what all the whispering and hushed voices and the "**big people talking**", "**mind your own business**" warnings had been about.

And after finding out the truth, I didn't really feel like eating much at all any more; fast food, or slow food, or any kind of food.

18

THE CAMERA

I will never forget that night. The night, during the half-term holidays, when I found out there was something seriously wrong with Grandad.

When Mum thought we were all asleep, and I was on my way back from a night-time wee, I overheard Mum in her bedroom speaking quietly on her phone to Godmother Patsy.

They weren't laughing and joking like they usually do or talking about people they fancy on the telly. They're especially always swooning over some actor called **Idris Elba** and going all giggly and girly whenever they see him. Grown-ups are such an embarrassment!

Anyway, I was straining to hear what they were saying, and I could only pick up the odd word. Mum and Patsy were switching between speaking in Jamaican patois and English like they usually do, and from her tone of voice I could tell Mum was serious.

She was talking about Grandad Bobby. It sounded like she was saying something about him having a camera. Maybe he'd won it! Perhaps that's what all the secrecy was about? Grandad hadn't won a certificate, but a prize?

But then Mum didn't sound excited. Why not? I'd wanted to have my own camera for ages — as well as a phone, but I knew, unlike Evie, that I wouldn't be getting one of those yet.

So even though I'd been eavesdropping, I couldn't get it off my mind. Something wasn't right, I just knew it. I had to ask Mum and Dad what was going on.

So, the next morning at breakfast I asked them, "What's so wrong with Grandad Bobby getting a camera? None of us are going to take it and break it."

I thought my parents were going to tell me off for listening in on the phone call or for my attitude-y question, but they didn't. They just stopped what they were doing and looked at each other in the way that people do when they've been caught out keeping secrets.

The Twinzies were sitting at the breakfast bar, having a race to see who could eat their cereal the fastest.

"Peter and Lena, now that you've wolfed that down, can you go into the garden and give Grandad's flowers some breakfast too?" asked Dad. "Can I rely on you to fill up your watering cans by yourself at the outside tap, without making a swamp?" Dad's eyebrows arched in a very questioning way at that bit.

The Twinzies sat up to attention like well-behaved puppies and nodded their heads furiously. They were just too cute.

Dad smiled and saluted them. "Go to it, my watering soldiers. Be brave, be strong. Don't get wet."

The Twinzies giggled, returned a salute to Dad and skipped off happily. I almost told Dad to get the towels ready, but I wanted to get back to the camera story.

I looked at Mum, who was now standing at the kitchen sink. Sensing my eyes on her, she turned to face me. Mum's eyes looked like they were about to spring more water than the tap.

"Is everything all right, Mum? I'm sorry I asked about the camera. It's okay if Grandad hasn't got one. I thought he'd won a prize, another award, that's all."

Mum walked over to me and cupped my face in her hands. She started smiling and tears began to swell in her eyes. "No, Sunny darling, Grandad Bobby has...well...he...he..."

"He has cancer, not a camera," Dad interjected, rubbing Mum's back gently.

At the time, I still really didn't take it in. I'd heard about cancer and seen adverts on the telly for charities that were trying to raise money to help get rid of it, but no one I knew had ever had cancer before. So now it felt like an unfriendly alien had landed a **great big spaceship** in the middle of our house and we didn't want it here.

My Grandad Bobby was ill, so very, very ill, and I'd

been too wrapped up in myself to notice.

"**Grandad will be all right, Mum, won't he?** He's as strong as an ox, that's what you always say. Right, Mum?"

Mum tried hard to smile, and stroked my face. "That's right, Sunny Sunshine, he's as strong as an ox."

It took at least a day for the news about Grandad to sink into my brain. All the things that had been happening over the past few weeks — months, even — began to make sense. Grandad's increasing tiredness. Losing his breath and holding his side underneath the tree that day he took me to school, after I'd cut my hair. Losing his **ox–ness**. The green mush that Mum kept making. My parents not being able to concentrate enough to do anything with their usual energy. Why, oh why did I think they were planning to surprise us all with Grandad's new certificate or that Grandad had won a camera? The clues were there all along. Silly, silly Sunny.

Life seemed to speed up very quickly from that point. It was hard to catch my breath.

Over the next few days, my parents told me what had been happening. They had no choice, as I persisted in asking them question after question. No more dismissing me by telling me that "**big people are talking**" or "**this is big people business**".

I made sure to ask questions when **the Twinzies** weren't there or weren't listening. I didn't want to upset them. I wanted to shield Peter and Lena from the agony of knowing. In trying to shield them, I understood why my parents and Grandad hadn't told me. They were trying to protect us all.

But now there was no turning back for me. This is what I found out:

Grandad had had an intensive course of radiotherapy a few weeks before, where he'd gone to the hospital every day for five days to try and shrink the tumour (the thing growing inside Grandad and making him ill). The doctors wouldn't cut the tumour out because they didn't think Grandad's body could take an operation like that at his age. Charley's mum had been trying to help with advice, because she's a nurse — that was part of the reason why she and Charley had come round for dinner that day.

Mum was also trying different remedies, like rubbing herbal oils into Grandad's skin and liquidizing and blending Grandad's food to encourage him to eat while he'd lost his appetite, giving him all the nutrients he needed to help fight the cancer. It was the first time in my life I was grateful for Mum's nutritious food. Anything, even all that green stuff, to help Grandad.

I set to work helping Mum chop up fruit and vegetables such as avocados, cucumbers and spinach to add to Grandad's special smoothies, and then I sat with Grandad to encourage him to drink. We took gulps together and he laughed as he saw my face shrivel up as I held my nose and swallowed. It wasn't the booming laughter of my grandad of old, but I knew I was helping him, I just knew it, as a flicker of a twinkle came back to his eyes.

We could do this — we could help make Grandad better.

Dad said that Grandad's generation is tough. "If Grandad could get through some of the hardships he's had to face in life, then he's got a fighting chance. The older generation have been through more than you or I could even imagine:

war, rationing, 1970s fashion, all kinds of storms. The point is they're strong and, by the grace of God, Grandad Bobby will get through this." Dad smiled softly.

I took hope from this, but it was plain to see that Grandad was getting weaker. Mum said the medicine Grandad took for the pain made him tired and dizzy and that was why he'd stopped taking us to and from school, even though Grandad had insisted he could carry on. But Mum and Dad had said no and changed things around at work to look after Grandad and us.

When I thought about it properly, things had started to become a little stranger every day. Sometimes Grandad didn't even know what time of day it was. When Grandad was well, everyone always knew the time because of him. He went for his newspaper at seven o'clock on the dot every morning. "Grandad is a walking, talking cockerel", that's what Dad always said. But for weeks we had been walking around like ballet dancers on tiptoes so as not to disturb him, in case he was taking a nap.

Now I knew the truth — and being in the bedroom next to his, I listened out for every creak of his bed and the groan in his voice as he changed position, trying to get comfy. And the dark circles around his eyes were deepening. But Grandad only joked and said, **"I'm just like Kung Fu Panda, without the moves or the big belly."**

I wanted to ask Grandad *How do you feel?* because that's what I'd noticed grown-ups saying a lot when someone is poorly.

So when Grandad was staring at **The A-Team**, one of his favourite old TV shows that he would sometimes watch with **the Twinzies** and me, I asked him, "How do you feel, Grandad?" And then I realized that grown-ups probably ask that question because they don't know what else to say, like when they ask someone if they want a cup of tea or start talking about the weather.

Grandad looked up from the screen and said, **"I feel like a car driving along the road with one wheel."**

You could always rely on Grandad to say funny things to make you laugh, but this time I wasn't laughing, and neither was he.

I held Grandad's hand and squeezed it gently. Without looking at me, **he squeezed mine back** ever so gently too.

19
LETTERS FROM ACROSS THE ENGLISH CHANNEL

I went back to school after half-term feeling a little bewildered. Like I had lived a completely different life in that one week away from school. All the bad dreams and lack of sleep were catching up with me. It didn't feel like I was returning from a break. I just felt so tired. My hair hadn't greyed, I didn't need to use a walking stick, not even wrinkle cream, but somehow I felt older. Frailer.

I told Arun and Charley what had been going on, behind the games area at lunchtime. Charley bowed her head and rubbed at her eyes. When she lifted her head, her cheeks were bright red and her sky-blue eyes had a rainy film sweeping across them.

Arun rubbed my shoulder. **"Your grandad is sooo strong, Sunny,"** he said, removing his hand from my shoulder and flexing his arm muscles. "He'll be fine. I can't wait for him to see my **Holly/Bolly mash-up** at the assembly."

I smiled weakly. I'd forgotten all about the assembly. What had seemed so important before half-term now held no interest. Maybe Miss Peach had been talking about it in class that day. I don't know. I hadn't really been listening to anything. I'd numbed out. I think I remembered muttering something to her about reading a poem.

"Are you okay, Sunshine? You don't look well," said Evie at the end of the school day.

"I'm fine," I said, closing her down. The last thing I needed was one of Evie's backhanded-compliment put-downs.

But the next day at school, as I walked into the classroom, Evie tapped me on the shoulder and gave me a piece of white card. I turned it over. On the front was scrunched-up yellow tissue paper glued to the top of a green pipe cleaner. I think it was meant to be...a sunflower?

Maybe a tulip? I'd finally found Evie's weakness — she wasn't that great at art.

I opened the card to find a simple message written inside. **I hope you feel better soon. I'm sorry if I've upset you. Sometimes I say things without thinking**, it read. My exhaustion lifted. My heart transformed into a butterfly, its little wings fluttering in my chest. I looked over and met Evie's eyes. She smiled that brilliant smile of hers. I bit my lip, in the way you do before you start to cry. "Thank you," I whispered. I sat down, warmed by Evie's kindness, confident now that we could fix things between us.

"Settle down, children, we have some good news," said a very excited Miss Peach. "We have received letters from France!"

Suddenly, a cold shiver shot down my spine, puncturing the warmness I'd felt only seconds before.

Miss Peach tipped a big brown envelope upside down and the letters from across the English Channel tumbled onto her desk like milk pouring onto cereal.

She tapped her fingers together gleefully. I've never

seen anyone react that way to an envelope unless they know there's money in it.

"But which one to read aloud first?" she said.

The class held their breath. I nearly started hyperventilating. What did she mean, **Which one to read aloud first?**

Miss Peach closed her eyes, rummaged through the pile, plucked a letter out at random and held it up triumphantly — just like it was **a winning lottery ticket**.

"And...the...letter...is...for..." said Miss Peach, holding on to each word and savouring their release (all that was missing was a drum roll), **"Sunshine Simpson!"**

I think I died in that moment.

"Sunshine, come to the front of the class and have the honour of reading out the first letter," trilled Miss Peach.

"Can someone else have a go?" I asked, trying not to sound ungrateful. It didn't work.

"No," said Miss Peach firmly. "First out, first served."

"Why do we always have to be on show?" I muttered

a bit too loudly. "What I mean is, Miss, I thought we'd be able to read our letters by ourselves, **privately**, later."

"Yes, most of you will. We won't have time to read out all the letters, but you have pulled the lucky straw. What an honour to be able to share yours with your classmates."

Well, yes, but no. I didn't **want** to read the letter in front of everyone. Alarm bells rang loudly in my head at what Elise Baptiste's reply might say.

I stole a look over at Evie. Her eyes shone, looking at me expectantly. She nodded for me to go on. Bossily or helpfully? Who knew? **Who cared!** I was now dreading having to open that letter. I could almost hear it ticking down to the explosion.

Gulping down a huge ball of air, I somehow moved my leaden legs to the front of class. Perhaps it wouldn't be so bad? It was almost exciting, even. Like reading a brand-new, straight-out-of-the-printer's Jacqueline Wilson novel, I tried to convince myself.

As long as I didn't do or say anything stupid. As long as nothing Elise Baptiste had written gave my secrets away.

I wasn't going to be **Silly Sunny**. I was determined

to be **Sophisticated Sunny**. French people are very sophisticated. There was hope.

I cleared my throat and looked down at Elise Baptiste's reply. It felt like each word was jumping out of the page at me. I refocused. I could do this. I was ready.

"Dear Sunshine,
Comment ça va? (How is it going?)
Merci beaucoup, mon amie! (Thank you very much for being my pen pal.) You have a wonderful name. Trop cool! My friends all smiled when I told them you are Sunshine (we say le soleil in France)."

I paused and looked up into the radiant face of Miss Peach. She oozed with pride. She nodded encouragingly as I tried to pronounce the French bits in the letter. I cleared my throat again before continuing.

"Your Grandad Bobby and your best friends Charley and Arun sound très gentils. My grandmama is Scottish.

I have a friend who is a pain and very annoying. His name is Olivier Leclerc. Bête comme ses pieds! (This means he is as stupid as his feet!)"

"If you'll pardon my French, Miss Peach," I said apologetically. My stomach began to knot.

Miss Peach seemed confused, which was probably for the best.

I wondered if I should make up the rest of the letter, or faint to get out of reading what was about to come next. Fainting wouldn't have been hard. The words on the page started to swirl before me and when I looked up at my classmates **it was like a scene from one of my nightmares.** Their faces moved back and forth in kaleidoscopic vision.

I could see a few more words in French, so hopefully no one would understand what they meant. Unless Evie had done a crash course in French on her visit to Paris (it wouldn't have surprised me). There was nothing else to do but read quickly, in the hope that neither Miss Peach nor any of my classmates — Evie in particular — would catch what I was saying.

"Your Evie sounds très énervante! Yes, like an ant crawling on your back and you cannot reach far enough to get rid of it..."

I heard sharp intakes of breath, like the whole class had been sucked into a vortex.

Unsurprisingly, I didn't get to read the rest of the letter because Miss Peach stopped me in my tracks, yanking it from my trembling hands. Her golden smile had soured into a frown and she gestured with a pointed finger for me to sit down.

"May I remind you, children, we want to give the French students a pleasant taste of what life is like in the United Kingdom; we do not want to put them off before they even have a chance to reach our shores. Nor do we want to give them the very *wrong* impression that we are unkind to each other — or that our school is plagued by irritating ants — because that is *very* much *not* true!"

Miss Peach flashed me a look.

"Sunshine, I do not know what has got into you. Perhaps you should stay in at break to write back to Elise and give her a rather different impression of life at this school?"

There was no **perhaps** about it. That was my **breaktime** sorted.

"And I think Evie deserves an apology, as she is clearly and understandably very upset," added Miss Peach.

I couldn't protest. I had to swallow my pride and say sorry in front of everyone. "Sorry, Evie," I whimpered.

My classmates mumbled to each other and I could hear their snickers. Evie rubbed at her eyes as if she was on the verge of tears.

I wasn't just Silly Sunny, I was Bad Sunny. I'd messed up in front of everyone yet again. I hate to think about it even now. Not just my humiliation, but Evie's. It was an awful thing to do. Grandad was so right when he said, **"If you spit at the sky, it falls back in your face."** Now I knew exactly what he'd meant.

The butterfly that had fluttered in my heart now felt like it had been sunk to the bottom of my stomach by a giant stone. I felt sick as I made my way back to my desk — but not as sick as I felt after what happened next.

20

LE FIGHT

At lunch, Evie came over to Charley, Arun and me in the playground. She wasn't going to let this one go — I could tell by the scrunched-up look on her face. She had Izzy and Maya with her. For backup, I assumed.

"Well?" she said.

"Well what? Don't expect me to apologize again. I've already done that in front of the **WHOLE, ENTIRE CLASS!**" I did feel terrible, really I did. Evie and I had only just kind of made up before I read out Elise's letter. But I ended up fronting it out, which made things so much worse.

"I should have known **your smart mouth would get**

you into a whole heap of dumb trouble one day," said Evie, almost snarling at me. Had she even meant the sorry she'd written in her card?

Our truce was over. We were both now kicking our white flag of surrender into the dirt.

"You've barely known me for two minutes, so how would you know?" I shouted.

I was sick of Evie thinking she knew everything about me. Only Arun and Charley could ever talk to me like that. Not that they would, because they were proper, **real** friends.

"What have I ever done to you anyway?" asked Evie. "You were nice to me when I first started school."

Hello? Had I fallen asleep and woken up in a different story? She really didn't know why I'd be upset with her? I let out a huge sigh. "Okay! I'm **sorry**, Evie. You obviously want me to say it again, so there you have it. I don't know what else you want me to do. **I am Silly Sunny. Does that make you feel better?**"

Evie pouted and folded her arms. "Well, yes, **you are silly and mean**. And I'd be very surprised if Miss Peach even allows you to perform in the jubilee assembly now. Mind you, I don't suppose it would make much of a difference, as *you haven't thought of anything interesting* to do yet, have you? Oh no, what was it you said to Miss Peach — a poem? I hope it's original, because even your letter was about me!"

Izzy and Maya tittered. I always think people titter when they are caught in a slightly embarrassing situation and don't know where to put themselves.

Before, when Evie talked to me, I wasn't quite sure how to take it, with that sweet little voice, almost like she was reciting a nursery rhyme. But this time I did know. She wanted to humiliate me, like how I had humiliated her in class. Thoughts of the card she had made for me disappeared into a red haze. It was the final straw. I erupted in a rage.

"I don't want to be in the stupid jubilee assembly anyway! With your big head in the way, I wouldn't even be able to fit on the stage! **All you do is diggity-dig at me.** Yes, you do get on my nerves. You are worse than an irritating itch. You are insufferable and unstomachable. And I don't care whether unstomachable is a word or not!

Stop pretending to be my friend. Friends don't act like you do. Go and pout like a fish somewhere else. I'm sick of looking at you and hearing your screeching voice. **Just leave me alone!**"

I heaved, breathless at my words. Arun, Charley, everyone looked shocked.

"How dare you! How dare you speak to me like that! I'm going to tell Miss Peach."

"Tell her then. I don't care what you say to me any more."

I turned to walk away, exhausted and upset from my outburst.

"I'm amazed you found any words to say," she shouted angrily. **"You usually run to your grandad for everything. Where is he anyway? Is he dead or something?"**

It was the worst of blows.

All fell quiet.

No one else at school knew about Grandad's illness except for Arun and Charley, and I'd sworn them to secrecy.

I swung back round to face Evie. Her face had drained

of colour. My face felt like it was turning bright purple. Something snapped inside of me: maybe it was my heart splitting in two, my ribs cracking or my blood vessels popping. **Cymbals, drums and tambourines played in my head, and my whole body shook with the noise.**

Without thinking, I charged at Evie like a bull that had just seen a big, red flag.

I pushed her. She flew backwards, falling into a puddle. Evie's arms and legs flailed and flapped. She reminded me of an octopus.

"My coat!" she gasped. **"My mum bought me this coat! You've ruined it!"**

I stood there, blinking. A crowd had surrounded us; wasps joining a picnic. I felt so guilty. I moved towards Evie to help her up. But she quickly rose to her feet.

"Don't touch me!" she yelled. And she pushed me. Hard. I stumbled backwards, but didn't fall.

I heard Charley scream.

Then suddenly a hand yanked at me. Another hand did the same to Evie. She was pulled backwards and upwards like a puppet on a string.

Miss Peach and Mr Bayliss, one of the Year Six teachers, had stepped in. Miss Peach looked so shocked that Mr Bayliss had to do the talking.

"Mrs Honeyghan's office — now!" he shouted. The crowd dramatically parted as Evie and I were marched through.

What had just happened? Looking back on it, it felt like a blurry nightmare. Unreal. Why had Evie been so cruel and why had I been so cruel to Evie? How did we end up like this? Tiredness, panic and despair washed over me as I waited to hear my fate.

21

JAWS OF DOOM

Sitting on the plastic seats outside Mrs Honeyghan's office felt like the **loneliest** — and most **uncomfortable** — place to sit on the planet. Evie and I waited in silence. Mr Bayliss perched himself between us like he'd just been refereeing a boxing match and needed to sit down for a rest.

We were waiting for ages, but then the door to Mrs Honeyghan's office opened and we stared into **the Jaws of Doom**.

Peering into the dark unknown of the head teacher's office was quite a scary thing for someone who had never been in that much trouble before. It was a black hole! A cavernous cave!! **An abyss!!!** I won't go on. But I was panicking, and probably using too many exclamation marks.

Mrs Honeyghan looked stern. How angry was she? It was hard to tell. Mrs Honeyghan always looks like that, even when she's doing pleasant things, like singing hymns and playing the piano during assembly.

She came to the door, lifted her arm and gave a slight twizzle of her hand, gesturing for us to come in. Mr Bayliss got up, so we dutifully followed, even though I wanted to race down the corridor in the opposite direction, wailing and screaming like my bum was on fire.

Miss Peach was there, which settled my nerves a little, though she looked very flushed. **Things must have been bad** if both Mr Bayliss and Miss Peach had been called off playground duty.

Surprisingly, Mrs Honeyghan's office was actually quite cheerful and not a black hole at all — not as stern and serious as her. Colourful paintings that had obviously been painted by us pupils had been framed and put up in pride of place to brighten the greying walls.

I looked around, admiring my surroundings, and then

my eyes met Mrs Honeyghan's, which for a second looked like they were blazing **red**. But I think it may just have been her fiery **red** hair reflected in her red-rimmed spectacles, which, in turn, set off her bright **red**, yellow and green floral dress, and the big **red** ring on her finger. I made a mental note that **Mrs Honeyghan likes the colour red** — maybe a little too much.

"Are you listening to me, Karis?" asked Mrs Honeyghan.

"Yes, Mrs Honeyghan," I whimpered.

Evie gawped like a fish, staring blankly ahead, eyes wide and mouth half open, like she'd stop breathing if it shut. Her coat was muddy from the fall.

Mrs Honeyghan squeaked as she sat down in her red leather chair. **Yep, RED!** And I'm assuming the squeak was from the leather and **not from her bottom**, which, despite the trouble I was in, made me want to burst into a giggle. I think it was the nerves. Mrs Honeyghan soon wiped any hint of a smile off my face though.

She looked us hard in the eyes. Her stare was so intense that I had to look away. Evie didn't even flinch. She was as stiff as a plank of wood.

"Do either of you want to offer an explanation for what has happened today?" asked Mrs Honeyghan.

Mrs H paused for a few moments to give Evie and me a chance to speak. Neither of us said anything.

"I see. Now you have become united in silence... I should send you home immediately, girls. This school values patience and kindness as well as helping each student's character to thrive in positive ways. **Today, you have let your school and yourselves down.**"

I could feel my insides shrivelling up.

"But..."

We held our breath.

"I have called your parents and they have each given me some background information that might explain this sudden deterioration in your characters. And it is only for these reasons that you are both still standing on school premises."

Mrs Honeyghan spoke in short, sharp sentences that got the job done. "**I do not want name-calling** in my school. And I **certainly do not want physical altercations**. This is an educational establishment, girls, and not a wrestling school." She paused before continuing, "Besides, there is too much paperwork involved in fights."

Mrs Honeyghan raised an eyebrow and looked across at Mr Bayliss and Miss Peach. They gave the faintest hint of a smile. I think they had just shared what grown-ups call an **"in-joke"**, because Mrs Honeyghan looked quite pleased with herself.

"Is that understood?" said Mrs Honeyghan.

"Yes, Mrs Honeyghan," we both piped in unison.

"As I have said, if it had not been for the pressures your families are under, you would not still be here. And you would not be taking part in your class's jubilee assembly, nor the school disco."

Out of the corner of my eye, I could see Evie's lips starting to twitch and quiver.

"However, in light of the fact that Miss Peach speaks so highly of you both, and your extenuating circumstances, you will be allowed to stay at school and be involved in the celebrations."

We both breathed a huge sigh of relief. Who would have thought I'd be grateful to still be taking part in the

Golden Jubilee assembly? And what was this about **extenu-thingy** circumstances? What did that even mean? This opened up a new mystery.

Mrs Honeyghan cleared her throat for her dramatic finale. "I know you are both very good students, even though I find it hard to believe that two intelligent people would disgrace themselves in such a way. However, if I so much as hear a whisper of any more problems, **you will both face severe consequences**. Is that understood?"

"Yes, Mrs Honeyghan," we called.

"And now..." Was it time for a dance? A hug? A sing-song? No, it was much worse than that.

"**An apology** is called for — from both of you," declared Mrs Honeyghan.

"Sorry, Mrs Honeyghan," we both chimed.

Mrs Honeyghan clapped her hands together, probably half in frustration and half in amusement. "No, not to me, girls, to each other."

Not again! I hadn't recovered from the apology for the Elise Baptiste letter.

We were statues, mouths clamped shut. Our

stubbornness wouldn't allow us to budge.

Mrs Honeyghan's nostrils quivered. I imagine that's what a dragon does too before it sneezes out a ball of flames. Something told me that Mrs Honeyghan, when she's riled, is not as sweet as honey.

"Let me help you," she said firmly. "Karis…Sunshine… you first." Mrs Honeyghan tapped her fingers together so that her long, red fingernails sounded out an up-tempo beat.

I looked at Evie. Her body was taut and upright, like a soldier on parade. All that was missing was the salute.

I had to get it over and done with quickly. **"Sorry,"** I said in a flash. Mrs Honeyghan shot me a look. **"I'm sorry, Evie,"** I said again, hoping that I had spoken more meaningfully this time. It must have been enough, because Mrs Honeyghan immediately swung in Evie's direction.

"Evonne?"

She'd just added insult to injury — Evie would have hated Mrs Honeyghan calling her by her proper first name.

Evie's head turned stiffly towards me as if it needed oiling.

"Sorry, Sunshine," she whispered hoarsely. Perhaps her voice needed oiling too.

"Right then, good! Tomorrow is another day. I wish you and your families well — and I look forward to your assembly performances at the end of term. That will be all, girls."

Mrs Honeyghan waved her hands towards the door, sweeping us away.

Evie looked straight ahead, refusing to look in my direction, but I stole a glance at her. This wasn't the sparkling Evie I knew. She looked like she'd had all the air sucked out of her. And I wasn't enjoying it. Not even one bit.

From what I could pick from the bones of what Mrs Honeyghan had said, it seemed that Evie had her own problems to deal with — just like me.

I was in shock. **I'd been having bad dreams, yes, but this was a real-life nightmare.** Why was everything going so wrong around me?

Worse still, Mrs Honeyghan had called either Mum or Dad to let them know what had happened. Which meant, even though Evie hadn't managed to kill me, whoever picked me up from school would probably finish the job.

22
FLOAT LIKE A BUTTERFLY

It was worse than I'd feared, I was met by **double parent power! Both Mum and Dad picked me up from school.**

I didn't know what to say. How could I repeat the words that Evie had said about Grandad without upsetting them? How could I tell them what I had written in that letter about Evie?

"Sunshine had a fight with Evie Evans," called Lena Twinzie, announcing the news practically as soon as Mum and Dad's feet hit the playground.

"Yeah — and she got locked up in the smelly mop cupboard as a punishment," bellowed Peter Twinzie.

"Right. Just to be clear, I pushed Evie and she pushed me back. It wasn't strictly a fight — and there were no cupboards or mops involved in my telling-off," I told **the Twinzies. The Twinzies** shrugged and ran off. That's what happens when gossip starts spreading — the truth gets rinsed to death in a smelly, old mop bucket.

Fortunately, Mum and Dad seemed to be taking what happened in their stride.

Instead of the stern looks, talk of never buying me anything again as long as I live, and crumpled faces that I'd expected, we walked home in near silence. Not the kind of silence when you know your parents are so cross with you that they can't speak and they'll deal with you when you get home. It was a calm quietness. More of a gentle breeze than a rugged wind.

My parents asked no questions, they simply held my hands: one hand each. It was like being in the middle of a mum-and-dad sandwich. I half-expected them to start swinging me through the air after every few steps until their arms grew tired, like they used to when I was younger. But now, clearly, wasn't the time for games like that.

The Twinzies ran ahead of us, squealing and shouting, overexcited at having both Mum and Dad pick us up from school, I guess.

On the walk home, people called out and asked about Grandad: Mrs Flowers the florist, Mr Chanda at Chanda's Groceries, Jakub at the Polski Sklep. But instead of their usual smiles, they wore worrisome frowns. And, of course, Mrs Turner was on patrol at her front gate. "He's not too bad," Mum and Dad said to everyone, but they said it in a funny way, unnaturally, through hurried smiles and stiff faces.

Grandad was in the living room, sitting in his comfy old chair with his feet on the pouffe, watching a cowboy movie. He had a snack of hard dough bread and condensed milk on the side table next to him, one of his favourite treats. It's not my cup of tea, but it made a change from the green gloop Mum — and now I — tried to feed him. But he had barely touched it.

Without looking at me, he held out his arms. I hurried over and he enveloped me like he was holding on to the best present ever. When we finally let go of each other,

I sat next to him, by the side of his chair, and for a little while we watched the goodies chasing the bad guys out of town.

"You know, I've had a few battles in my time," he said once the adverts were on. "Did I ever tell you about the time I worked in the States?"

I looked at him quizzically.

"America. The land of the free!" said Grandad.

I shook my head. I knew Grandad had worked in America, of course, but he never said much about his time there. He shuffled in his seat, making himself as comfortable as he could.

"Before I came to England, many of us from the West Indies went over to America on a government contract to work as farmhands. I was in sunny Florida first. Florida is the place of alligators and golden shores — but I didn't see much of those." Grandad's talking brought a series of short, sharp coughs from his throat. He put his hand out to indicate that he was fine and I waited for him to settle back down. I wasn't going anywhere. I didn't want to leave his side.

"We cut cane in Florida...sugar cane, tall and long. If you made a mistake in the fields and went into someone else's row and cut theirs, they were grateful but they wouldn't help you with yours. You had to go back and do your own row as well."

"That was a bit mean, wasn't it, Grandad?" I said.

"Ah, it's one of the many lessons you learn in life: **keep an eye on what you're doing and don't be a fool**. There's no fool like a young fool, trying to be the quickest and the best!" Grandad laughed and then coughed again. "I worked in Indiana too — picking tomatoes in field after field. Then there was Connecticut, picking tobacco."

"Which one was the best, Grandad — the cane, the tomatoes or the tobacco?"

"The best?" said Grandad thoughtfully. "I'm not sure there was any best — apart from being out in the fresh air. It was all hard work, but it was work that we needed to do to help provide for our families back home. But I can tell you, it was in America that I almost met a sticky end."

"What happened, Grandad?" I blurted out, fascinated.

"We were in the fields and taking a water break. 'Come

and look over here, quick,' shouted one of the guys and we all ran over to see what it was. It was a snake. 'It gwarn bite you. **Ssssssss...**' hissed the guy, and we all laughed. A bit of humour, you know, broke up the day. Then, in a flash, one of the supervisors was on us. He came right up to me, into my face, as close as you are to me now, grabbing me around my throat. I think he chose to pick on me because I was the shortest. I could feel the saliva from his mouth fly into my face as he spoke. **'What you laughing at, boy?'** he spat."

Grandad was really confessing now.

"I couldn't help myself, I felt my right hand fly up." Grandad balled his fist. Despite his thinning arms, Grandad's hands were still as hefty as hams. "And you know what, Sunshine? Before I could stop myself, I hit him square under the chin. I knocked him out cold. **BOOF!**"

I sat bolt upright. "And what happened then, Grandad? You must have got into terrible trouble! Did they send you to prison like **Nelson Mandela**?"

"No, no." Grandad smiled. "The other supervisors swooped in on me."

I gasped. "Huh? And what happened then?"

Grandad squinted. It seemed like the memory was as fresh as if it had happened yesterday. "To be honest, I thought I was done for. A lot of Black people who lived in America at that time suffered some terrible racism. Not only name-calling but getting physically hurt. But being Jamaican, and maybe because we'd come over on this deal with the government for us to work, seemed to help my cause. They didn't physically harm me, they just took me straight to the airport and sent me back home on the iron bird. I didn't even have the chance to gather my possessions together."

"That's terrible, Grandad! That man was so mean to you. You were only joking around."

"Sometimes people don't like the unknown or difference, Sunshine. They find it threatening." Grandad sighed. "There's a long, hard history. A lot has changed, but there is still much work to do. Hopefully, by the time you've grown, the problems will be gone. **Hope springs eternal, sweet Sunshine, hope springs eternal.**"

Grandad smiled warmly. I smiled back.

Listening to Grandad hurt my heart. I don't understand

why some people don't like you, just because your skin looks different to theirs. **Why does having a different skin colour make such a big difference to some people** or make them think they can treat you as less than them? It's ridiculous. Hate is so hateful. And stupid.

Then I thought about the problems I'd caused closer to home, because of my dislike of Evie Evans, and sadness flooded my heart along with the hurt. "I'm sorry, Grandad," I said. "I'm sorry for letting you down."

Grandad reached for the remote control and turned the TV over to the horse racing. "I've never been too lucky with the horses," he said. "But I struck lucky with my children and grandchildren. Never change, Sunshine — but **do your best not to let others draw you into trouble**, you hear?" Then he switched the TV off and cuddled me.

"**Did you float like a butterfly and sting like a bee?**" he whispered.

"No, Grandad, I'm not **Muhammad Ali**."

He laughed and pulled me tighter to him. "No, maybe not like the great man himself, but maybe like his great-granddaughter."

"Or maybe just like you, Grandad," I giggled. He smiled, but looked exhausted after our chat. I nestled further into his chest as gently as I possibly could and we said nothing more.

That evening, as I lay in bed, everything that had happened earlier raced through my mind. I retreated under my duvet, trying, hopelessly, to escape from the memories.

Everything was wrong. Grandad was sick. Evie hated me. It didn't even matter now about being uninteresting. I would rather be uninteresting or silly than so horribly **sad**. And all the extra stress I had caused Mum and Dad and Grandad — it was just unbearable to think about.

I heard my bedroom door creak open and from under my duvet I could just see the landing light illuminating a square patch on my carpet.

Footsteps.

"Is anyone in there?" There was a knock on my bedside table. It was Mum.

She gently lifted the duvet from my head and sat

down next to me on the bed.

Could things get any worse? I should have known Mum wouldn't be able to resist telling me off.

I sat up, but looked down, twizzling my thumbs back and forth.

"So…" said Mum, trying to sound casual, but also twizzling her own thumbs. "What's up?"

What's up? Had Dad been giving Mum emergency lessons in how to not completely freak out!

"Well, I kind of had a fight, Mum."

Mum half-choked (probably out of anger) and half-laughed. "I am quite aware of that, Sunshine. We've practically had Mrs Turner at the doorstep with a reporter's notepad and pen in search of a scoop!"

I guess that was Mum's way of trying to lighten the situation, but I didn't know what to say.

"Why didn't you tell me things were this bad?"

"They weren't. I could handle it."

"Well, forgive me, but from where I'm sitting, it doesn't look that way."

Now, this sounded more like Mum. She saw my face

start to crumble. She changed course.

"Friends bicker, but this? I know you, Sunshine. Usually, if you have a knock, you get up and go again. You find a positive way out."

"Well, there is clearly nothing positive about me."

I hadn't wanted to go through it all. The letter. What Evie had said about Grandad. Luckily, I didn't have to.

"Well, you know I spoke to Mrs Honeyghan on the phone this afternoon, and Charley's mum called me a little earlier too."

Charley had sung like a canary.

Two canaries, it seemed. She'd spilled all the details of what had happened to her mum. And then Charley's mum had told my mum.

Mum shook her head, trying to fit the splintering pieces of the jigsaw together. **"But...Evie tries to call you all the time.** I don't understand where this has come from."

I may have forgotten to mention that bit. Yes, Evie

tried to call me quite often, but I'd started to avoid her calls as the weeks went by, pretending I was on the loo, helping **the Twinzies** with their homework or assisting Grandad in the garden — anything rather than talking to her. I didn't want to, even though I was supposed to be helping her, because every time we spoke it made me so cross.

I gulped at the thought of what had happened with Evie and my eyes brimmed with tears.

"I've not come to lecture you, Sunny. I think you already know that **fighting never solves any problems**. If anything, it only multiplies them. And Evie shares responsibility for what happened too... I just want to understand, that's all."

This made a change. Mum usually reacts first, calms down later. But I was too choked to speak.

Mum patted my knee through the duvet. "There's a slice of Granny Cynthie's cake waiting for you downstairs if you want it? She baked a sponge cake to cheer us all up."

Ah, my lovely Granny Cynthie could whip up a cake standing in the middle of a snowstorm.

Still, I said nothing.

"Well, I'll save you a couple of slices." Mum smiled and rose to her feet. But her back wasn't held straight and tall as she made her way to the door. The way Mum usually carries herself makes her look double her size, like a proud robin. Instead, her back was stooped, as if she was carrying a boulder on it. That was my fault. I knew I was responsible for knocking all the stuffing out of her.

"Thank you for not being angry. I know you don't need this right now."

She turned to face me. "To be honest, when I got the call from school, of course I was upset. This isn't like you. But then I remembered — **we all make mistakes**. Your grandfather reminded me of the time I tried to pour glue into my mum's shampoo bottle when I was around your age, just like Matilda supergluing the rim of her father's hat. But I stuck my fingers together instead. Your grandad caught me red-handed — or should I say **glue-handed**?" Mum smiled.

I gasped at the thought of Mum doing anything so naughty — and the fact that she'd actually just told a joke.

"It's how we learn from our mistakes that helps

us grow. Goodnight, sweet girl. Tomorrow is another day — and we will deal with whatever it brings together. And, Sunny, **ssshhh**...don't tell anyone about the glue. That's between you, me and Grandad. Okay?"

She winked. I winked back. Mum and I had never shared a wink like that before.

23

STRICTLY COME FIGHTING

The next day, Grandad tried to raise my spirits before I set off for school. **"Walk strong. Be strong. Do your best. No one will ask for more,"** he said.

He lay back on his pillows in bed. I fist-bumped him gently, and went on my way, warmed through to my toes by his words.

Grandad was having good days and bad days. Good minutes and bad minutes. Saying things you could understand and then saying things that didn't make any sense.

One time, Grandad could see people coming out of the wallpaper. He started talking about people I had never heard of. People he knew from Jamaica and when he'd worked on the buses, Mum and Dad said. It was like Grandad's body had been taken over by a younger him, who was reliving his past. And it was scaring me.

Along with the biting worry about Grandad, I was also gripped with fear of how things would be at school.

But school wasn't what I'd expected.

Evie and I were famous – like pop stars! The story of our battle had grown and risen like bread dough overnight.

"Everyone thinks there's going to be a rematch because the fight was broken up so quickly — that's the word on the playground," said a very excited Arun at break. "If it wasn't for Charley screaming and drawing so much attention to it, then there probably would have been a clear winner!" Arun sounded like a sports commentator.

Charley blushed.

"Dylan Singh, Izzy James, Brett Bryan, Matthew Akinrinlola and Maya Watkins say Evie won. And Foley Thomas, Seraphina Adebayo, Dominika Kamińska, Riley Edmunds and Carey Crick say you won."

Arun rattled off the names like he was reading out the class register, barely pausing for breath.

"Yes, yes," I interrupted, dismissing him like I wasn't interested. I tipped my head to one side. "Anyone else pick me?"

"No. I don't think so," said Arun. "But Riley Edmunds and Carey Crick are like the equivalent of four extra people. If anyone knows about fighting it's those two — so extra props to you. That kind of unofficially makes you the winner — on balance."

"Oh, really?" My stomach flipped a little with excitement. In that moment, I conveniently forgot the desperate look in Evie's eyes when we were in Mrs Honeyghan's office, and about all her troubles, whatever they were. I even dumped from my brain what Mum had said about never winning when fighting — or whatever.

"Imagine if you had round two with Evie, it could be like *School Fight — The Sequel*," said Arun.

Charley, hot on his heels, joined in too, even though she doesn't like fighting. "Yeah, like *School Fight*...like *School Fighter*...like *School Fight*..."

"Like *School Fight 2*?" I helped.

"Yeah, like *School Fight 2*," confirmed Charley, like

she'd just invented the best film title ever.

"What about *Strictly Come Fighting*? Or *I'm a Fighter...*
DON'T Get Me Out of Here?" said Arun.

I rolled my eyes as my two friends fell about laughing.
Were they for real? "It was more of a scuffle than a fight,"
I said, throwing water on their fire. I was beginning to feel
uneasy. **I didn't want anything like what had happened**
the day before to happen *ever* again.

I wanted to be interesting. I wanted to be exciting.
Popular even. But not this way. I'm a lover not a fighter —
and I said as much to Arun and Charley.

Plus, Mrs Honeyghan had warned us: any more trouble
and we'd be out of school faster than sweets out of a jar
left in a classroom full of kids and no teacher. Well, she
didn't say it like that exactly, but nearly.

"We know," said Charley. "We just got a little bit
overexcited. We don't want you to get into trouble again
— nor Evie."

"Did you see Evie's face in class? It looked like she'd
turned to stone," said Arun.

I nodded. I'd tried to say an awkward hello to her on

our way out for break, just to test the waters. Something to try and start making amends. Evie had looked as pale as a ghost and hadn't even registered that I was there — like *I* was the ghost! In fact, if I'd asked Evie for a rematch there and then, I'm sure I could have blown on her and watched her break up and float away like a dandelion clock.

I wondered if I should phone her. Maybe...later... no... it would be pointless.

And there was the jubilee assembly to worry about. I had work to do. I'd said to Miss Peach that I was going to recite my poem, and she was anxious to hear it. I wasn't surprised, considering what had happened when I read out the letter the previous day.

But then I remembered how truly awful my poem was. Thoughts of **Pizza is my sister, it's better than getting a blister**, flooded back into my mind.

I was on the road to embarrassing myself in front of everyone yet again. **I needed to speak to Grandad.** I needed his inspiration. I needed his help.

24

DREAMS

After school, the air was warm, being June, but the general mood was chilly. The direct opposite of the warmth I'd felt from Grandad that morning. Mum had been supposed to pick **the Twinzies** and me up from school, but where was she? Dad had arrived late — hot and flustered, stuttering an apology to Miss Peach. No word of an explanation to me. And where were **the Twinzies**? I didn't get a chance to ask, because Dad was on a call, whispering down the line to a mystery person all the way home.

I dawdled behind him, craving any crumbs he might throw me. *How was your first day back at school since you nearly lost your life at the hands of your mortal enemy?*

What is wrong with your mortal enemy? What is wrong with you? I don't know. Say anything, Dad. But Dad wasn't interested in me, he was talking on the phone with one hand and scratching his bald head with the other. He barely noticed I was there.

An uncomfortable ball, burning like fire, was swelling inside of me, somewhere between my stomach and my heart. Ripening to bursting point. Silently waiting. I needed to talk to Grandad about how I was feeling. It was only Grandad who ever truly understood.

The house was uncomfortably silent when we arrived. I ran around opening and shutting doors, calling for everyone to come out. Were we playing a secret game of hide and seek? If we were, I didn't feel like playing right now. Or had everyone just left in disgust, the shame of what I'd done finally catching up with them?

"Where's Mum? Where are **the Twinzies**? **And where's Grandad? I need to talk to him**." The ball swelled up to my throat. I couldn't breathe. Something was wrong.

Dad slipped his phone into his back pocket, held my hand and led me to the living room. We sat down on the sofa and Dad pulled both of my hands into his.

"You're having a rough time, I get that. But right now I need you to be calm, and I need you to be the bravest you've ever been. Can you do that for me?"

I tried to steady my breathing, to make it slow and deep instead of rapid and panicked. That's what Dad tells Mum to do when she's getting mad about Auntie Sharon or her mother. "What? Braver than the time I trapped my thumb in the door and there was all that blood and my nail came off?"

"Yes, indeed." Dad smiled and bit his lip. "**The Twinzies** are at after-school club."

"Why?"

"Well, we just needed a bit of time to sort things out and we wanted to speak to you first, so that you wouldn't worry."

This only made me more worried. "Sort what out? What's happened? Where's Grandad? Where's Mum?"

Dad held my hands a little tighter. "Well, you know Grandad Bobby is poorly?"

"Yes, he has cancer," I said, trying to be grown up and matter-of-fact about it.

Dad squeezed my arm.

"Well, it…" I could tell Dad was finding it hard to say the "C" word, almost as if it was choking him like how it was choking Grandad. "Well, it's spreading."

"Spreading?" I imagined the cancer being spread like butter across Grandad's body. "Can the doctors stop it spreading?"

"They've tried, but it hasn't worked, and now the cancer is causing Grandad too much pain." Dad gulped. I gulped.

"So that's why he's struggling to get up and down the stairs? Grandad says it's like he's trying to go uphill and the wind's sending him downhill, '**like I'm trying to climb Mount Everest**', that's what Grandad says."

"And I imagine that's exactly how it does feel. Grandad knows how to set the scene all right."

Dad fell quiet.

What was he trying to tell me? Why didn't he just spit it out? I feared my nightmares were coming true.

My latest dream had been really frightening.

As soon as I'd drifted off into sleep, everything about it

had felt so real. I opened the door into Grandad's bedroom, but the light switch didn't work and I could only hear Grandad's voice calling to me in the darkness. Trying to be brave, I stepped into the room to find him, but as soon as I did, **I realized there was no floor, just more darkness.** And I plummeted like a cartoon character. Except that I didn't fall into the ground with a great crash, I kept tumbling into nothingness. And then I woke up, sitting bolt upright, too frightened to move or say anything.

It was a relief to see Grandad again the next morning. A bit weaker, but still there.

Every day since I found out Grandad was ill, I would touch his shoulder, brush my hand over his grey bristly hair, tug gently on his fuzzy beard, or fiddle with his ham hands. I just needed to make sure Grandad was still real. Still here. "What? You tink you see a ghost?" Grandad would say, and then wiggle his sausage fingers and toes to prove he still existed.

But now, where was he? Where was Grandad?

I was frightened to ask but I had to. "Is...has Grandad died?"

"No, no," said Dad quickly, horrified that he'd kept me in such awful suspense. "Grandad is in hospital. He has an infection. And sometimes infections can make you a bit disorientated...a bit confused. Your mum and your Auntie Sharon are with him."

"You mean, that's why Grandad started talking about random things as well?" I asked, remembering the incident when Grandad saw people coming out of the wallpaper.

Dad nodded.

Knowing Grandad was safe in the hospital made me calm down. **"So when's he coming back?"** I asked, feeling a bit more upbeat.

Dad hesitated. "You see, Sunshine, Grandad is very poorly and weak now — and it's getting harder for him to cope at home. It would take a good while for us to convert space for him downstairs, and he'd be isolated upstairs, especially when none of us are in the house. So when Grandad comes out of the hospital, he'll be going into a hospice."

"A what?" I exclaimed. Whatever it was, it didn't sound like Grandad was coming back home at all.

"A hospice is a bit like a hospital, but more of a home away from home," Dad explained. "There will be nurses and carers who can look after him properly. He'll have his own room, with a window and a chair."

This, to me, was now utterly, completely ridiculous. "He has his own room, and a window and a chair here. We can look after Grandad at home!"

"I'm sorry, Sunshine. No one has thought about the situation more than your mum and me. And we've come to the decision that this, unfortunately, is for the best."

"For the best?" I got so hot I thought I might explode, like the sun was beating its sticky hands down very hard on top of my head. Like the ball of fire that burned within me was suddenly going to burst from my stomach and scorch the whole world.

"'**We've** come to the decision?'" I shouted. "Well, no one asked me, and I bet no one's asked **the Twinzies**. Just because we're kids doesn't mean we don't have opinions! Not that you're interested, but my opinion is you're horrible and mean. You all want to get rid of **MY** grandad."

And before I realized what I was doing, I started

shaking uncontrollably, not like a leaf, but like a washing machine on a turbo-charged spin cycle. Dad pulled me in towards him, burying my head in his chest. Dad didn't tell me off, and he didn't say **We know best** like grown-ups usually do in a roundabout sort of way. All he said was "I'm sorry, I'm so sorry", almost cheeping like a frightened little bird. And he sounded so helpless and lost that I just burst into tears.

25

MARY SEACOLE HOUSE

Grandad went into the hospice that weekend, and Mum and Dad were finally going to let **the Twinzies** and me visit him the following week.

I was desperate to see him. I wanted him to come home and for life to be **normal** again, but everything felt so out of control. My classmates were starting to practise their jubilee assembly pieces for Miss Peach. She was so good with me, because she knew all about what had been happening at home. I was running out of time, as the assembly was only a few weeks away — but all I could think about was Grandad.

Mum tried to warn me. "Grandad Bobby is very poorly now. And I've been um-ing and ah-ing about whether to take you to see him...but I think you need to. It's time... it's time to see your grandad."

Grandad's hospice looked a bit creepy. Mum and Dad had made it sound like it was going to be a gingerbread house, not something transported directly from Transylvania.

The Twinzies craned their heads to look up at the top of the building in awe.

"Wow!" said Peter Twinzie. **"I bet Spider-Man couldn't even climb those walls."**

He was probably right — or his spidey outfit would be shredded to pieces, at least. The building was tall and made from red bricks. Sharp bits on the roof stuck out like jaggedy teeth in need of a good dentist. And its big red double front doors were like two giant lips that could swallow you whole.

On top of the giant lips, chiselled into stone, were the numbers 1862. "That's when it was built," Mum told us.

The outside of the building made me think there could still be a few people living in it from 1862, which made me feel all shivery.

"Are you cold, Sunshine? Let's get you inside," said Mum.

But then Mum stopped as she was ushering us past a blue sign with white writing that said, **Mary Seacole House. Welcome.** A great, big scary welcome, that's all I can say.

"Do you remember anything about Mary Seacole, Sunshine?"

This wasn't the time for one of Mum's trips down memory lane. I almost sighed. I just wanted to see Grandad.

"Yes, yes. She was a nice old Jamaican nurse. She liked to travel and she gave sick soldiers medicine made from herbs during the Crimean war and helped them get better. She was very brave." *The end.* I didn't say the "**The end**" bit — I didn't want us to be marched back home again. **"Can we go in now?"** I asked, impatience starting to bubble over. Mum nodded.

I walked through the red-lip doors, half-expecting to

be eaten alive — but I've never been more surprised. I blinked my eyes a few times just to be sure.

The building didn't look scary or miserable inside, it more resembled a space station. Bright white walls blended in with bright white floors like a sea of milk. The reception desk greeted us in forest green, a little island bobbing along on the milky ocean, while paintings of all different kinds of flowers were dotted around to bring the walls to life.

A glass conservatory lay beyond the reception desk. Mum said this was the "day room" where all the guests of the hospice came together to do activities like drawing and painting and to talk to each other.

Grandad wasn't in the day room, which was a bit strange, because Grandad had always liked to have a laugh and a joke with people. Grandad liked "**good company**". I made a mental note to ask him why he wasn't using it.

We walked over to the reception desk, where a woman dressed in a blue uniform beamed at us. "And who might you be?" she asked **the Twinzies** and me, like we were one person. She put one finger to her lips and pretended to think hard about it. "Yes, you must be Bobby's grandchildren, Peter, Lena and Sunshine."

"How did you know that? **Are you magic?**" asked Lena Twinzie, suspiciously.

The nurse smiled and tapped her nose. "No. But I recognized the twinkle in your eyes. Just like Bobby's. I bet you have no end of tales of mischief that this lot get up to," she said to Mum with a laugh in her voice.

"Don't I just. There's truly no end," said Mum, raising her eyebrows.

I smiled, which the nurse immediately noticed.

"Yes, the smile is definitely like his too," she said, looking at me. **"And I'm guessing your grandad's just the person you want to see right now?"**

"Yes, please," I said eagerly.

While the nurse, Mum and I walked, **the Twinzies** decided to try and have a sliding competition along the glossy floors, pulling Mum along like they were huskies as she tried to rein them in.

Then up we went in the lift. I usually get excited in lifts. I pretend I'm going on a magical adventure. But this time it didn't feel like a trip in Willy Wonka's elevator. I was excited to be going to see Grandad, yes, but worry gnawed and nibbled away at me too.

There was silence, until a sudden noise, followed by a familiar smell, ripped through the air.

"Pardon me," said Peter, giggling.

"Peter!" shouted Mum, all shocked and embarrassed, which made Lena start giggling uncontrollably.

"But Grandad says, 'Let wind be free wherever it be, for that was the death of Mary Lee'," said Peter to justify his actions.

I told them both to shut up, which made Mum tell me to shush, which made me cross. I huffed and folded my arms.

"I'm so sorry," said Mum to the nurse.

"Don't worry," she laughed. **"I'm not sure who Mary Lee is, but that's a very good point."**

Thankfully, at that moment the lift's doors shot open, as if it desperately wanted to spit us out. I half-expected Mum to press the button to go back down to the ground floor and then run screaming straight out of the front doors, because of us embarrassing her, but she didn't — she gritted her teeth, held on tight to **the Twinzies**' hands and told us all to "**Come on**".

We walked down another long, glossy corridor. Nurses passed us and nodded and smiled like they knew who we were. Mum was here every day, I knew that, during her lunchtimes and straight after work, so she was probably a very familiar face. I also knew Mum was tired: her eyes were red and droopy and sad-looking, like she hadn't slept in days and days. She probably hadn't.

I tried not to stare into each room. Mum says it's rude to poke your nose into other people's business. If Mrs Turner was with us, she'd have been **all over this like Paddington Bear on a marmalade sandwich**.

We whizzed past each room so quickly that I could barely get a look in anyway. As the end of the hallway approached, there was only one door left. **The Twinzies** let go of Mum's hands and shot straight ahead into the room. She raced in after them, followed by the nurse. I gulped.

I was desperate to see Grandad — but then again, was I? Why were my feet no longer moving? Doubt chewed away at me and I wanted to kick myself for being so silly.

There wasn't a **grizzly bear** or a **wild dog** on the other side of the door, it was just Grandad: my wonderful, cuddly, funny friend. But I was afraid. How could I fear my own grandad — my best friend?

I bit back my fear and walked in. Grandad's room wasn't like his familiar bedroom at home, with its bright colours, awards, pork-pie hats and black, gold and green Jamaican flag hanging proudly over his bed. These walls were painted white like the rest of Mary Seacole House, and one small painting (of flowers again) hung there looking a bit lonely without any other friendly pictures to hang out with.

There was a big, rectangular window criss-crossed with strips of wood, but these didn't stop the light from streaming in; the swaying trees outside cast dancing shadows on the floor. A tub of **paper flowers** sat on the windowsill. Someone — perhaps Grandad — had made them from bright tissue paper and fashioned the stalks out of green pipe cleaners. The flowers reminded me of Evie's card. Maybe Grandad had made the flowers in the day room with the other "guests"? I couldn't help but think that any passing bee would be sadly disappointed. "No nectar here," they'd say and buzz off.

Then I heard his voice. Not the booming voice I knew, but a tired whisper that sounded like it had been carried here on a long journey. As I glanced to my right, I saw him — a teeny-tiny version of Grandad Bobby lying in bed. He looked so fragile, so weak. I couldn't bear it. The nurse fixed his pillows and then smiled warmly at us as she left the room.

"You na see me?" Grandad whispered hoarsely. *"Yes, mi know, I'm the Invisible Man."*

He tried to laugh, but instead it came out as a wheezing cough.

Even **the Twinzies** sat down quietly in the corner of the room, as if they had summed up the drama of the situation and instinctively knew they needed to behave. They started to get to work on a jigsaw puzzle that Mum had randomly produced from her handbag.

Grandad's eyes rested on all of us, one by one, but his limbs didn't move. His feet peeped out from beneath his blankets and his arms rested on two pillows laid either side of him. Mum tried to re-cover his feet and body to keep him warm, but Grandad kept trying to swat her away like an annoying fly. *"Leave mi nuh, Cheryl,"* he whispered.

I would have laughed at their antics (it felt a bit like being normal again) if it wasn't for the fact that when his bed sheet slipped down from his chest, I could see his ribs sticking out of his skin, arching like a bridge.

Grandad Bobby wasn't the Invisible Man, like he'd joked. I could see him and hear him all right and he was still here, just about, but I didn't like what I saw. He looked like he'd been eaten alive. Grandad Bobby looked like a stick man.

My eyes darted over to Mum. I needed help, but she was shuffling awkwardly and busying herself trying to give Grandad sips of water through a straw. For the first time in my whole life, I realized that Mum was at a loss for what to do or what to say.

Grandad must have known this too because, from somewhere, he managed to summon enough energy to speak. He gave a lopsided, knowing grin. "I like your hairstyle, it looks nice. You're a wonderful girl, Sunshine.

Never change. And nuh worry about your assembly, **just do your best. No one will ask for anything more. Have your adventure, sweet Sunshine. I'll always be proud.**"

I smiled and touched my hair. It was growing back, but it was still a little uneven. That never mattered to Grandad, he always accepted me for who I am.

Right there and then, Grandad looked like he'd used up every ounce of energy, as if he would splinter into a thousand pieces if I touched him but, in that moment, I couldn't help but rush to him, gently wrap my arms around his delicate shoulders and hug him, though he couldn't easily lift his arms to hug me back.

"Thank you, Grandad," I said. **"Thank you for everything. I love you."**

26

NINE NIGHTS

A few days later, Grandad Bobby had gone.

"He's passed away…"

"He's gone to live with the angels…"

"He's gone to heaven…"

Lots of people said lots of things in lots of different ways to say that Grandad had died.

"Grandad's infinity!" said Peter Twinzie, shooting around the room with one arm outstretched into the air like he was about to take off and fly. I managed to raise a little smile at the thought of Grandad as a beam of light never ending and always being there.

As if to outdo Peter, Lena Twinzie stood up and

declared, "I'm going to give Grandad a hug in God," and she wrapped her arms around the air, hugging the emptiness like Grandad was right there with her.

Grandad's dead! Grandad's dead! That's what I heard over and over again in my head. I wanted to bury myself underneath a pile of pillows to try and stop myself from thinking it. Why couldn't I have nice thoughts like **the Twinzies**? But I just couldn't. I was angry. I was furious that this nasty, mean sickness had stolen my grandad from us. I couldn't shake the sadness. I was sinking in it.

And then we had to be sad in front of everyone else, because we were having a "**nine nights**".

Basically, what I found out is that a "**nine nights**" is a Caribbean tradition that we do when someone dies. Lots of relatives and friends come around to the house of the person who has died for nine nights afterwards, "**to give the family support and comfort and to pay their respects**" — that's what Dad and Auntie Sharon said anyway.

Mum moved around the house like a tornado, cleaning every crevice and corner. Nowhere remained untouched by her feather duster and mop. She shouldn't have bothered, because by the time the hordes of people had traipsed through, she was back at square one with the wiping and hoovering.

Dad said we could've had just one night where we'd hire a hall for everyone to come and pay their condolences, but Mum said that people would still turn up at the house anyway because Grandad was so popular.

Time whizzed by as **the Twinzies** and I travelled from home to school and back again to a house filled with visitors. It was all a blur. At the end of the days of nine nights visits, we were exhausted. But everyone had been so kind to my family, bringing boxes of **tea**, jars of **coffee**, crates of **juice**, and **sweets** and **biscuits** for us kids, and **whiskey**, **rum** and **beer** for the grown-ups.

We also had **mountains of food**: curry patties, fried fish, jerk chicken, rice and peas, curried mutton, and on and on with all the Caribbean delights we could wish for. Jakub from the Polski Sklep even brought Polish bread and sausages and **traditional Polish cakes**. And Mr Chanda came with loads of supplies from his grocery store. Arun and his parents brought a stack of vegetarian **pakoras** and **samosas**, and Charley and her family came with a home-made fruit loaf called a **barmbrack**, an Irish apple cake and a packet of chocolate digestives (**my favourite!**). My biggest surprise was seeing Evie's dad. He handed over a huge bottle of **Jamaican rum** and some soft drinks for us kids. But there was no sign of Evie.

Mum, Auntie Sharon and Godmother Patsy offered out food and drinks on trays, shooting between each room on invisible roller skates.

Sometimes Auntie Sharon would take a break from being the "**hostess with the mostess**", as Dad called her, to win a few of the games of dominoes that were being played, and to have "a drop of rum" in between. And Mum just rolled her eyes.

But, most of all, it felt like **everyone who came to visit us cared**.

The funeral was held at the start of July, on a scorching hot day, and it was even busier than the nine nights.

I didn't realize that Grandad had known so many people. There were coaches of visitors who arrived from who knows where. Some people also flew over from Jamaica, America and Canada. But there was no Grandma. We had tried to call her home in America and Mum and Dad had even contacted Grandma's sister in Jamaica, but no one could find her. "Who knows where in the world she is," blustered Mum. So we had to carry on without her.

At the service, Mrs Flowers the florist recalled how Grandad laughed his head off when he first heard her name. And Mr Chanda told everyone about the day that Grandad had foiled the robbery at his shop. He stood at the front of the church, wiping his eyes with his handkerchief, and recalled how Grandad Bobby had saved not only the shop, but his life too.

Mr Chanda said he was "so proud to know Bobby and to call him a friend. He was a man of great dignity...of great dignity." And then he burst into tears.

Mrs Turner cried bucketloads as well. Poor Mrs Turner, she loved Grandad too.

I'd never been to a funeral before. On the telly, they always seem sad and lonely things with everyone walking around in black — black shoes, black suits, black dresses, black hats — and lots of sobbing and wailing into handkerchiefs.

Despite all our tears, we called the funeral a send-off, because it was definitely **a celebration of Grandad's life**. And most people wore blue, not black, because blue was Grandad's favourite colour.

The Twinzies and I wore sky-blue and everyone said we looked brighter than the summer's day itself. Auntie Sharon wore purple, and Auntie Sharon and Mum had a **"little discussion"** because Mum said Auntie Sharon **"never sticks to the script"**. Even Dariuszkz wore a smart, light-blue suit and tan shoes instead of his usual uniform of hoodie and trainers.

In the evening, we held a party for Grandad. It sounds strange to say that, because we were so sad, but it was important to continue the celebration too. More stories were shared about all the funny things Grandad had said and done, and all the kind ways he'd helped other people. My heart swelled so much that I thought it was going to burst. The ball of flames I had been carrying for so long felt less thirsty. Grandad always enjoyed a good party: music, people, joy, laughter. He would have loved this send-off. I just wish he could have been here to see it.

27

BRIGHT AS A BUTTON

When Grandad's send-off was over, I'm not going to lie, it was hard to adjust. All the relatives and friends, and the people I had never seen before, said their goodbyes and wandered back into their own lives, and it was so quiet in our house.

The Twinzies squeaked around like mice. Mum wasn't boiling and stewing things to death, she was burning them instead. Granny Cynthie and Grampie Clive scuttled in and out to help in the garden and with cooking the meals, probably because they didn't want Mum to poison us or accidentally burn the house down.

When Grandad died, **the Twinzies** and I had a few days

at home — and we were off for the funeral, of course — but then we went back to school.

Arun and Charley kept me going by chatting away about ordinary, everyday stuff, and Miss Peach was so kind in letting me sit things out whenever I felt sad or overwhelmed. I didn't even have to practise for the assembly, which filled me with great relief, because I had zip-all to present. Plus, I kept out of Evie's way and she kept out of mine. It was like we had an invisible agreement to give each other space.

After school, I would come home and cry. Into Grandad's favourite chair, into my pillows, into the garden — anywhere that would take my tears.

I felt bad for my parents. I knew they wanted life to feel normal for us again. Even though normal wasn't normal any more. Our normal had changed.

Mealtimes were probably the hardest. I could hear every chew as we sat and ate at the dinner table, just Mum, Dad, **the Twinzies** and me, like we were making our own orchestra of food sounds: slurping, biting, swallowing. It was unbearable. I don't think Mum could bear it either, because one evening she broke the silence.

"You had a phone call earlier, Sunshine…it was Miss Peach," she said.

Everyone looked up in surprise. Maybe because someone was attempting conversation, which at least made us all stop chewing.

"How did she get our number?" was all I could think to say.

Mum frowned.

"What I mean is, why did she call?"

"She was checking on how you are."

"Oh! That's nice of her." I said, relaxing a little.

Mum still had a funny look on her face. "But…" she added.

"But"s, I've grown to understand in all my years on earth, never lead to anything good or anything you want to hear.

"But…**she also wants to know whether you would like to take part in the Golden Jubilee assembly**. She says you've not wanted to rehearse with the others. Miss Peach will understand if you don't, but she doesn't want you to miss out either, and thinks it might be **good for your confidence**…and just…just to **take your mind off things**. Your father and I were deliberating whether or not to just sit you out, but we felt it should be *your* decision. And, don't forget, there's also your end-of-term school disco. I know that Grandad would always want you to have some fun." Mum smiled.

As "**we**" decisions never usually included me, I was grateful that they'd at least asked. On the other hand, panic began to rise. I started shaking my head, like a horse trying to escape its bridle.

Dad rose from the dinner table, stretching out his arms as if to say, **Whoa, horsey**. "Sunshine, you are as bright as a button, funny and gregarious. Maybe this would be just the boost you need? But we also know it's very soon after Grandad's passing, and you shouldn't feel any pressure to do it."

I was not feeling as bright as a button. More like a very dull, unpolished one.

"I know I've been going on and on about the show. But I don't think I can do it," I said.

"You have been going on a bit lately," agreed Peter Twinzie. "But not about the show. You haven't been rehearsing properly for that *at all*."

Mum, Dad and Lena flashed him a look.

Peter swallowed down his food with a giant gulp. I couldn't blame him: the chicken was slightly burned and tough.

"No. I definitely can't do it. Not without Grandad here. Grandad was trying to help me...to cure my **lost–voice–itis**...and **I can't do this without him now**. I can't!" All my words started to trip over one another, jumbling into a mass of sorrow.

"Sunny, Sunny, Sunny," said Dad, now kneeling at my feet and looking into my eyes. "You and your grandad had a very strong bond, an unbreakable bond. You're grieving. It's natural to feel all sorts of things, but I want you to know that Grandad Bobby loved you and **the Twinzies** very, very much — and you loved him. Nothing will ever change that. And we understand if you don't want to do the show. That's absolutely fine. Just know we are here for you. Whatever any of you need, Mum and Dad are here for you."

259

Lena started to cry. Peter hugged her and started to cry. And then I started to cry too.

We couldn't eat any more, and as we moved into the living room, Dad took out his phone and started playing one of Grandad's favourite tunes: a song called "**She's Royal**" by a Jamaican singer called **Tarrus Riley**.

"He always said that you and Mum and Lena were his Nubian queens." Dad smiled, and then he bowed like we really were queens and he and Peter held out their hands like old-fashioned gentlemen inviting us to dance.

Our tears gradually changed to smiles as we twirled and danced to the reggae beat. At the end of the song, Mum stopped me spinning, held my shoulders and looked into my eyes. "**I want you to feel confident enough to be you**, like your grandad always encouraged. Even if you do get the occasional telling-off." She smiled. "We love you. I love you. Nothing is ever going to change that."

My spirits lifted. I thought about Grandad. He always loved a good performance and a great show. What would he say to me now?

"Just do your best, no one will ask for anything more.

Have your own adventures." His last words to me.

"Okay," I said, still sounding a little tentative. "I've changed my mind. I want to try and do the show, but I just haven't been happy with any of my ideas. I can't get it right. Something's missing."

Dad's lips spread into a broad beam. "We've all been off our game, that's understandable, but tonight has given me an idea that might inspire us all…"

A spark of hope lit my heart.

28

THE SHOW MUST GO ON!

"Are you sure this is a good idea?" Mum asked Dad. "I don't know if she's ready. I don't know if any of us are ready. Maybe she just needs another pep talk, instead of something so...so elaborate."

It was Saturday evening. Mum, Dad, me, **the Twinzies**, Grampie Clive, Granny Cynthie, Auntie Sharon, Dariuszkz, Godmother Patsy and even Mrs Turner were all squashed into the dining room with our best clothes on.

In the days leading up to this, we had all been charged with thinking of a performance for our very own family talent extravaganza.

Dad had said it would **"help to get our creative juices flowing"** for the jubilee assembly **"and help us to focus on something other than sadness"**. Dad got himself so engrossed in the project that the look of excitement on his face was creating a rumble of nervous energy amongst us. In my case, the rumbling was in my tummy. I'd hardly eaten anything all day due to my stomach flipping over and over. If I felt such nerves at the thought of performing in front of my family, how on earth was I going to stand up straight and perform in front of everyone at our school — and the one in France?

"It may be rough, but we are certainly ready," announced Dad at the start of the show. **"AND now presenting...Britain's Got the Simpsons, in honour of our father, grandfather and friend, the irreplaceable and irrepressible Grandad Bobby!"** Dad threw open the double doors between the living and dining rooms with all the flair of a ringmaster at a circus.

The drama matched the setting; the living room had been transformed into a wondrous place of beauty.

We all walked through the doorway, which now

dazzled with a beaded curtain. Our mouths opened wide in amazement.

The ceiling was equally splendid. White stars and paper lanterns looked to be floating near it, and a glitter ball was in the centre, like the moon had come down from the sky to visit our living room. The window was draped with a banner graffitied with the words **WELCOME TO THE SHOW** (created by Dad and Dariuszkz). White spotlights danced across the wooden floor.

Grandad's picture took pride of place on the mantelpiece, its frame covered in silver tinsel, next to the Sunshine-was-born-in-a-taxi photo.

"WOW!" said **the Twinzies**.

Mum brought her hands up to her mouth like she was about to pray. "It's **beautiful**, Tony," she gasped. "So, so beautiful."

"Shizzaam!" exclaimed Auntie Sharon. "This is making my rooms look plain."

Auntie Sharon has leopard-print wallpaper and a matching rug in her bedroom, along with zebra-print paper and matching rug in her lounge. That's all I can say.

264

"You've been busy, Tone, in that little man-cave shed of yours, haven't you? Not just using those digits for crunching digits, eh? Who knew your boy had such talent?" Auntie Sharon said to Granny Cynthie and Grampie Clive. Granny and Grampie's faces lit up like lamps.

Dad double-shuffled his eyebrows and put one finger to his lips. "I'm also a secret lemonade drinker...ssshh..." he whispered. Mum, Auntie Sharon and Godmother Patsy laughed. Don't ask me! They were probably sharing one of their **"big people"** in-jokes about something from the ancient past.

"Sit down, sit down," said Dad, now in full ringmaster mode — all he needed was the top hat. Talk about getting into character. **"On with the show!"**

The sofas and coffee table had been placed in the dining room to give us more space. All that remained in the living room was Grandad's chair, as if he was still with us as the guest of honour. We sat around the edges on the dining-room chairs and extra garden furniture, all quiet in anticipation. Even Mrs Turner was quiet — this had to be a first!

"She may be small, but she's got it all! Presenting **the Great Lena-Stupendous, magician extraordinaire!**" cried Dad.

With all the excitement, I hadn't realized that Lena had gone missing. Out she came from behind the glittering curtain in a sparkly waistcoat and black trousers, carrying a black top hat. She looked so cute.

"Awww," came the call from the darkened room.

The spotlight fell on **Lena-Stupendous**.

"Now, for my first trick, a feast never seen before by any human eye."

A feast or a feat, we didn't mind.

"Woo!" shouted Dad.

"Woo!" we all shouted.

"Let's magic brown bunny from the hat."

Never been seen before? It's the oldest trick in the book! I kept my mouth shut.

Lena turned the hat upside down, back around, and banged the brim, just to convince everyone that brown bunny, her favourite toy, was definitely nowhere to be seen.

Dariuszkz was chosen to double-check that brown bunny was not there and knocked his head on the glitter ball in the process.

We could see a suspicious bulge in Lena's buttoned-up waistcoat, but no one said a thing. The cute factor was far too high.

"ABARACADABARAT!" she shouted and tapped the hat with a wooden spoon three times. Lena turned her back on us, wriggled a bit, and within a minute she had spun back round again.

"Can my trusty assistant now recheck the hat?"

Dariuszkz, lumbering over with his long legs and ducking past the glitter ball, **put his hand into the hat and pulled out brown bunny by his long floppy ears**.

"TA-DAH!" Lena shouted. Everyone clapped, with Peter clapping the loudest. Lena beamed.

Next up was Auntie Sharon.

She was going to sing the **Whitney Houston** classic, "I Wanna Dance With Somebody".

"Are you sure about this, Sharon?" asked Patsy. "We all know that singing Whitney has slayed many a giant."

Auntie Sharon pursed her painted red lips and flicked her long red plaits behind her back defiantly as she made her way to the centre of the living room, wearing a sparkly red mini dress and high heels to match. "Well, this giant ain't for slaying! **Hit it, Tone!**" Auntie Sharon kicked off her shoes and straightened her dress.

Dad slowly made his way to the sound system, making a sign of a cross twice across his chest as he went.

I wish I had asked for divine intervention too. I'm not sure whether Auntie Sharon was **trying to communicate with dolphins** in oceans across the world, but I have never heard such a high-pitched trill in all my life

and I never **EVER** want to hear anything like it again. It must have been like a repeat of fireworks night for all the neighbourhood pets. I'm sure I heard some dogs howling in the distance.

Dad looked shook. In fact, we all looked like we'd just experienced an earthquake.

"My work here is done," said Auntie Sharon triumphantly, clicking her fingers and re-flicking her hair.

I'll say. I doubt that any of us will ever be the same again.

"Moving swiftly on," said Dad. "Now for the father-and-son act, Double Trouble." Dad and Peter Twinzie did a quick change in the dining room and out they came in matching tracksuits.

Auntie Sharon whistled.

An old dance song with a fast beat started playing and coloured lights strobed across the room.

Dad and Peter started doing all kinds of street-dance moves: the robot; popping and locking; Peter did his version of a worm across the floor, which really did make him look like a fish out of water, he was flapping all over the place; and then Dad showed off his killer breakdancing move — he spun on the floor, doing some impressive windmills.

By the end of the display, we weren't sure whether to clap or call an ambulance.

"You know, **just thought I'd bust some moves from my youth**." Dad grinned, holding on to his side.

"Yes, just mind you don't bust your back in the process," laughed Mum.

Next up…

I couldn't believe it. Mrs Turner rose to her feet and came to the front. Dad pulled up a chair for her. We all looked on, open-mouthed. Did Mrs Turner have talent? (To be honest, did **any** of us have talent?)

The white spotlight shone on Mrs Turner. She opened her mouth and…well, the most beautiful sound came out.

Mrs Turner sang "We'll Meet Again". It's a song by a nice smiley old lady who was called Dame Vera Lynn. Dame Vera cheered up soldiers in the Second World War with her singing, and Mrs T wasn't doing a bad job cheering up her audience either.

"Yes, go on Dame V's understudy! Sing it!" shouted Auntie Sharon, swaying her arms above her head. **"TUUUNE!"**

Grampie Clive passed Granny Cynthie the handkerchief from his pocket and she dabbed at her eyes. "Your great-uncles served in the First and Second World Wars — so many lives lost." She sniffed. **The Twinzies** and I went over and hugged Granny.

"That was exquisite, Mrs Turner," said Mum after Mrs Turner had finished.

"Yes, well, I haven't felt much like singing since my Brian left. But anything for the memory of our Bobby."

Mum passed Godmother Patsy and Auntie Sharon the tissues.

And then I had the surprise of my life — it was Mum's turn. Mum doesn't like drawing attention to herself — a bit like me, but different. But she got up and cleared her voice. I could tell she was nervous.

"This is a poem that meant a lot to me as a teenager. It's called **'Still I Rise' by Maya Angelou**."

Auntie Sharon whistled again. **"Preach it, sister!"** she called.

Mum threw her a death stare, but then she smiled brightly, took the deepest of breaths, and read the poem passionately.

I'm not sure I understood all of it, but I think it was

about believing in yourself. **If people try and put you down, you get up.** You rise again, confident that you are you. Mum looked so happy when she'd finished, as if it had stirred up something inside of her. I don't know what — that was hers to keep.

I looked over at Dad's face. I am not into pukey, mushy stuff, but I have never seen him look at Mum like that before, like if he had all the diamonds and money in the world, they still wouldn't be good enough for her. My heart swelled.

"Ahem...and finally on the bill tonight, our star turn... Presenting Miss Sunshine Simpson!" said Dad, after shaking himself from his trance.

Dad had said that I should take part in the family show too, even though I protested at first. Like I didn't have enough to think about with the assembly! But, for once, he really insisted, so I knew I had to do it.

Now, don't think I opened my mouth and sounded like an angelic choir girl. Let's be real, I'm not saying I sing like Auntie Sharon, but I won't be getting a recording contract any time soon either.

But, when I'd thought about it, I knew what to perform, as it was a way of bringing Grandad into the show as well. I started to sing.

Dad put on the music track of Bob Marley's classic song "**Three Little Birds**" to help me along — or maybe to drown me out. But it didn't matter, because towards the end of it, everyone started singing along with Mr Marley and me — and **in that moment we truly weren't worried about a thing.**

We all whooped and hollered as the show closed.

I marvelled at my family. How did they manage to do all this? To create and rehearse in such a short space of time? Dad joked and said that it was the magical wonders of the internet and express delivery that had saved the day. But that wasn't true. Dad had done all this to try and help me, to build my confidence, to cheer us all up. My family took part without question or complaint. **My family were saving the day. My family were saving me.** I had spent so long thinking we were all boring and uninteresting. I was so wrong.

I looked over at Grandad's photo on the mantelpiece.

He looked like he'd been enjoying the show too. I smiled at him. And then I looked over at his chair. It still had the dent from where his bottom used to sit for all those years. In that moment, I smiled as brightly as the glitter ball hanging from the ceiling.

I didn't know if I could perform on a stage in front of all those people at school, but this had given me the courage to at least try. What's more, I finally knew what I wanted to do for the jubilee assembly. So maybe I could pull it off, with a bit of inspiration from my family, from my grandad and from the past. Maybe I could do it after all.

Charley was right, sometimes you've got to work with what you've got.

29

PO-STORY

I didn't have much time, but I was happy with what I'd finally managed to pull together for the jubilee assembly. Mostly, I just wrote what was inside of me. Things that had been stored up and locked away in my heart for the longest while.

Miss Peach had gone over my presentation the day before the assembly, probably with a magnifying glass, to ensure there was no repeat of the **France—enstein's monster incident**.

If no one told me to break a leg, I would be okay. I didn't want any thoughts of spills, trips or falls filling my head. I had to keep my mind on the memory of the family talent show, and Grandad, to drown out any negative vibes.

"Are you sure you're okay to do this?" asked a worried-looking Miss Peach before the assembly started. "Do you feel strong enough?"

I wasn't sure whether I did or not, especially with no proper rehearsals to speak of, but the memory of **the Twinzies**' cuteness, Mum reading Maya Angelou's poem, Mrs Turner's performance, Dad almost doing himself a terrible injury, and Auntie Sharon's incredible confidence in the face of such dreadful singing, made me feel stronger.

"Yes," I said. "I will try."

Miss Peach placed her hand gently on my shoulder. "Okay! **Break a leg, as they say in showbiz!**"

"Thanks," I gulped.

The rain seemed to be plaguing us this summer. Through steamed-up windows — caused by the heat, the rain and nervous energy from a bunch of very excited kids — we could see a long line of drenched parents, grandparents, aunts and uncles, and various other long-lost relatives, queuing during a sudden rain shower to get into the hall. The looks on their faces said something like **This better be worth it**.

The big screen was set up with a live Zoom link to France. Miss Binoche's curly blonde hair filled the screen and then she stepped away to reveal a sea of children waving enthusiastically, with giant grins on their faces. I wondered which one Elise Baptiste was, and which was Olivier Leclerc — the boy who was as stupid as his feet. But there was no time to ask — it was show time!

The assembly was going well, with a real mix of performances.

Arun's dance extravaganza, using a fusion of Bollywood dance moves to a soundtrack of bhangra beats and "Singing in the Rain", went down a storm.

Carey Crick and Riley Edmunds put on a non-contact martial arts demonstration that drew **oohs, aahs** and **wows** from the audience.

Marcus Cruickshank gave a spoken-word performance,

telling the audience about how his dad ensured they tried something new together every time Marcus spent time with him in the holidays, whether this was kayaking, or rock-climbing or go-karting. But the most special thing he'd enjoyed with his dad was making their own kite and driving for miles all the way to the Malvern Hills together to fly it. Marcus held the kite proudly in his hands as he told the story. The kite may not have been able to fly in the school hall, but Marcus's pride was soaring with every word he spoke.

I was second-to-last on the bill. And guess who was on before me? Yes, that's right, **Evie**! From the side of the stage, I watched her float up the steps effortlessly, not even looking down to see where she was placing her feet. Her hair was tied up as usual and she wore a bright yellow hairband embellished with a bow. And her lovely, summery multicoloured dress floated behind her like a silk scarf blowing in the wind. Evie sang, sounding like a nightingale, lark and all other birds that sing gorgeously. She dedicated the song, called "True Colours", to her family. I thought the choice was a little inappropriate, because she hides her true colours from everyone. I'm just saying! But, of course, she received a **rapturous round of applause**. And, to be fair, she deserved it. How was I meant to follow that?

Evie floated back down the stairs, not looking to the left or to the right, and definitely not at me. We were now strangers, like we'd never met all those months before, when we were eager and ready with the newness of getting to know each other. That seemed a lifetime away.

Evie went and stood at the side of the stage, started taking deep breaths, and then began quietly sobbing to herself — her chest heaving with all the silent tears and the deep breathing. Miss Peach rushed to her with tissues, patting Evie gently on the back to comfort her.

What was going on there? Surely Evie should have been like that before her performance and not after it if she was nervous? I could have done with a massive pat on the back to get me onto the stage, that's all I knew. I could feel my legs seizing up.

My thoughts returned to Evie. What was wrong with her? **She'd been AMAZING** — so I couldn't understand why she felt the need to cry. Part of me wanted to go over and tell her how great she'd been. ***No hard feelings, Evie, you were awesome.*** But part of me also wondered if this was an attempt to upstage me — maybe revenge for ruining her new coat during our fight! My see-sawing heart was still very much up and down about Evie. But I didn't have any more time to dwell on that right there and then. It was my turn!

Miss Peach nodded at me reassuringly.

I didn't glide up the steps to the stage as gracefully as Evie had. I must have looked more like I was trying to walk on the moon, with legs made of jelly. A sea of faces stared at me. Was it too late to make a run for it?

Just be yourself. Do your best, I heard Grandad saying in my head. So, I stayed.

Clearing my throat made the microphone crackle loudly, and feedback screeched through the hall. Some people put their hands over their ears. Was this a sign of things to come? I clenched my fists, my nails digging into my skin in terror.

That's when I spotted Mum, Dad and Auntie Sharon, a few rows up from the front of the families' section.

Dad stuck one thumb up, while holding his phone up in the other hand. He'd promised to take video footage for Granny Cynthie and Grampie Clive; they couldn't make it, as the cold weather was playing havoc with Granny C's knees.

Mum waved and smiled at me reassuringly. Auntie Sharon pumped her fist and shouted, **"GO GIRL!"** Mum flashed her a look.

The Twinzies sat on the floor near the front of the stage, as each class was allowed to watch the other classes' performances. Peter and Lena grinned wildly at me.

I smiled twitchily at my family and, still with clenched fists, I started to read my half-poem half-story.

"This is my '**po—story**'," I announced. Some of the audience looked around at each other, and some looked on with questioning eyebrows, wondering what I was going on about.

"It's a poem and a story. **I wanted to talk about why my family's history is important to me.** But I also wanted to read a poem dedicated to my grandad."

This seemed to be enough of an explanation and there were nods of agreement.

"**My name is Karis Sunshine Simpson**. I am ten years old. I was born in England and my heritage is Jamaican.

"Jamaica is known as the land of wood and water and its motto on its coat of arms is '**Out of many, one people**'.

"My grandparents come from a generation of people known as **the Windrush generation**. These brave people left their families and all they knew in Jamaica and other countries in the Caribbean between the 1940s and 1970s to come to England — but they didn't come for a holiday or to put their feet up.

"Many worked for the NHS, as bus drivers, in the armed forces, or in factories and other places they were needed. They came to help rebuild their 'mother country', Great Britain, after the Second World War — but they have never forgotten their roots and their land of wood and

water. Though some faced prejudice along the way —
including being called mean names or being told to go
back to the country they came from, even though they
were invited here in the first place — they stayed and
made a big difference. They helped Britain to be strong
again. But they are still proud Jamaicans, so I am a
proud Jamaican, because out of many, we are one
people.

"Today, in Britain, to commemorate and celebrate the
contribution of Caribbean people, the 22nd of June is
known as Windrush Day.

**"We have been a part of Britain's past for many
centuries, and we are a part of Britain's future."**

I looked up. No one was laughing at me. No one was
yawning. People were watching and listening intently. I
took a deep breath. Filling up with a sense of pride, my legs
moved from an all-out shake beneath me to a slight quiver.
My hands relaxed a little. I felt stronger. I continued.

After clearing my throat (this time away from the
microphone), I gave the audience a whirlwind tour of some
of the things I had learned from my family. Like how cool

it was that three Black women mathematicians helped win the race to space; about brave, life-saving Jamaican nurse Mary Seacole; and about the multitude of inventions all created or improved by Black people that Dad had excitedly told me about.

There were so many to choose from and I had to leave a lot out so I could get to the bit about Grandad.

"I wrote a poem dedicated to my grandad," I told the audience, "because there are a lot of great people in this world, no matter where they're from, but **my grandad is one of the greatest people to me**." I stood tall — stretching to the tallest possible height I could pull myself to (which is pretty tall). There would be no more stooping — not any more! My feet were now firmly bolted to the floor, and my head reached the skies, ready to tell everyone about Grandad.

"My grandad the ox:

My Grandad Bobby came from Jamaica,

On a ship called the Arosa Star.

People always spoke so highly of him,

And he was the greatest of them all, by far.

Our local shopkeeper says my grandad is a hero,

He stopped a man from robbing his shop with a gun.

He says my grandad was as brave as a lion.

And he will never forget what he has done.

My grandad, he got tired.

We said 'Wake him up' as a dare.

Because Grandad couldn't play with us any more;

we thought it was so unfair.

But Grandad kept sleeping, like it was winter,

like he was a bear.

Grandad's wings could no longer fly,

And then it was time to say goodbye.

Now we talk about Grandad and put our memories

in a special jar.

My grandad: the ox, the lion,

a for-ever-glowing star."

I paused and then said, "My family, my history, my heritage are important to me because they help make me, me... The end."

I gulped and looked up. There was silence for a few seconds. I wasn't sure whether that was good or bad. Then, out of the silence, the applause erupted — and I could see the children in France clapping on the big screen.

"Three cheers for Grandad Bobby!" I heard a voice shout out from the audience. I think it might have been Arun's dad.

"Hip hip..."

"Hooray!" came the response.

"Hip hip..."

"Hooray!" More people joined in.

"Hip hip..."

"Hooray!" sang the teachers, who sat around the edges of the audience.

I hadn't stolen everyone's breath with my singing voice. I hadn't wowed them with brilliant dancing or blown them away with my gymnastics skills. But I had told them about my family and where we come from, and that was enough. I didn't feel like Silly Sunny. Maybe it would take a few years to be **Sophisticated Sunny**, but now **I was Satisfied Sunny**. More than that, **I was Inspired Sunny** — and that was okay by me.

I smiled and bowed.

Charley was last onto the stage with her Irish dancing. I'd never seen her kick so high. And her feet moved so quickly in time to the music, as if she was jumping away from hot coals beneath her feet. Her shimmering green outfit dazzled like a beautiful gemstone against the spotlight. She brought the house down.

At the end of the show, Mrs Honeyghan came to the microphone and said, "**What a treat!** Thank you to all the children who showed us their marvellous talents in Year Five's Golden Jubilee assembly performance. As you will know, each class at Beeches Primary has had a chance to showcase their talents. And, Year Five, I have to say that hearing and seeing what is important to you and what makes you, you — your influences, your talents, your cultures — has been a joy. You have warmed all our hearts. Every child in this school will be placed on our celebration wall — as this school would not be the same without its pupils, and that deserves to be celebrated.

"What is most apparent is that **all of you here are members of this school community** — children, teachers, parents, grandparents and, not forgetting, our new friends in France. And the ones who cannot be here? Well, they have made an indelible impression on our spirits, our hearts and our minds, and we will never forget them. They will always be with us."

Everyone cheered.

Our families stayed behind after the show to congratulate us once all the other children had returned to their classes.

Auntie Sharon rushed up and swung me around. I was just grateful that she didn't break into Whitney or start singing about us being champions again, or, even worse, blow the whistle that was around her neck. Mum probably put a stop to that.

"**Wow! Well done.** You snuck in the poem. You didn't tell us you'd written that," said Dad.

I'd mostly gone through everything with Mum and

Dad so they could check my facts, but the poem was meant to be a surprise. I noticed Mum wasn't speaking. Was she angry with me?

Mum stepped forward, looked at my face, and then grabbed me into a hug. The worries of the world that had been weighing me down now felt like they were floating up and away, out of the school roof.

"I'm so proud of you. I could never have been so brave, so great, so awesome as that in front of everyone at any age, let alone ten, nearly eleven." She smiled. **"I knew you could do it."**

For once, Mum didn't try to bravely fight back her tears — she was almost choking on them instead.

"Of course she did. **She slayed it!**" exclaimed Auntie Sharon. "Look at her family stock. She ain't Grandad Bobby's granddaughter for nothing, you know. **Big up the Simpson/Williams crew!**"

Dad's face was beaming. "Aww, come on in for a group hug." And we all hung on to each other like we were never going to let go.

30

STICKS AND STONES

Everyone was on a high when we returned to class, basking in their own performances and praising each other for a great show.

"Can I have a copy of your speech?" asked Maya Watkins. "My mum and dad were on their feet clapping, so I know they'd really like to read it."

"Yes, of course, Maya." I grinned.

In fact, Charley, Arun and I ached from all the smiling we did that morning.

"I'm **NEVER** going to hide under a bush again," said Arun. "I loved that so much — and no one laughed at me."

"Of course they didn't," I replied. "You were **AWESOME**, Arun!"

Charley nodded in agreement. Arun started to blow air out of his top lip towards his fringe. Then he suddenly stopped, ran his fingers through his fringe instead and beamed.

"And I've never seen anyone move their feet so fast in my entire life," I told Charley. "How do you do it?"

"Really?" asked Charley. "I wasn't sure whether I was in time to the music. And I thought I'd missed some steps."

I gave Charley a big hug. "You were perfect," I said.

"Your grandad would have loved this, Sunshine," said Arun. "And your poem had everyone crying."

We all went quiet and looked down at our feet.

"Your grandad would want you to be happy, Sunshine," said Charley, suddenly looking up and breaking the silence. "Come on, what are we going to wear to the school disco on Friday?"

I smiled. I knew my friends were trying to cheer me up in whatever way they could, but it felt like it would take me a whole lifetime to recover from all the things that had happened that term — let alone turn my mind to the school disco.

By lunchtime, I felt exhausted. Miss Peach allowed me to stay in the library — well, the room dedicated to books known as our school library. I didn't feel like playing. Sometimes I want to have fun and play and laugh and run, and sometimes I don't. Mum and Dad say that from day to day, hour to hour, or minute to minute, your mood can change when you're grieving. But I don't like it. It's like being on a see-saw that won't stop and sometimes it makes me feel a bit sick.

But, right then, I had a mellow feeling, like an internal river of warm honey was running through me. Grandad may not have been physically there at the show, but **I am a part of Grandad and I know he will always be a part of me**, and that made me feel stronger. I opened, closed and stretched my mouth, touched my throat and then smiled. At least for now, my lost-voice-itis had gone. It didn't matter what anyone else thought — not even Evie Evans. I was good enough just being me.

"Erm. I quite liked your po-story." I heard a tiny voice say.

I looked up. I couldn't believe who was standing in front of me. I rubbed at my eyes to convince myself that the person was real and then I took a quick look behind me just to check they weren't speaking to someone else, but they were definitely talking to me, "po–story" girl!

It was Evie. She'd stopped crying, but her eyes still seemed a little clouded over.

"And I like your hair. Your cane rows look great. I want some too. I'm going to ask my dad to book me an appointment to get my hair done," she said.

I suddenly felt self-conscious. Since my hair-cutting incident and the run-in with Evie over my unicorn hair, Mum and I had been experimenting with different styles. But she had finally taken me to a hairdresser to get my hair professionally plaited in time for the assembly. It felt like it took hours and hours and my bum was a little numb from sitting for so long in the hairdresser's chair. But when the hairdresser had finished and I looked at myself in the mirror, a small smile had grown to a grin. I touched my hair proudly, feeling the intricate plaiting that looked like a piece of artwork, forming a beautiful bun on top of my head. I loved it!

Now I have all these plans in mind for future styles. I might add a few beads, just for some zip — or maybe combine some plaits with a bit of a bushy 'fro. There are tons of styles to choose from. I realize that now.

"Thanks," I said a little nervously, expecting a cutting comment to fly in — but nothing came back. "You know, you should wear your hair out of your ponytail more often too, **your curls are really pretty**."

"Really?" said Evie, almost surprised.

"Yes, really." I smiled. Evie smiled back at me and touched her ponytail.

"I didn't know about all those things you said in assembly... **My dad's from Jamaica.** He was born there and then came to live here when he was little. And my mum's dad is from the Caribbean too, from Trinidad, but my grandma is from here. She's white. Dad calls us a happy blend." Evie smiled again.

"I know. Well, I knew that about your dad. Your dad

chats to my grandad about **'back home'**…I mean, used to chat to my grandad," I faltered, my eyes filling with water.

Evie changed course. "Yeah, they talked about cricket…and Jamaican recipes…like…like ackee and saltfish."

"I don't like ackee and saltfish," I suddenly volunteered, wiping at my eyes. "I can't believe it's the national dish of Jamaica."

Evie wrinkled her nose. "Is it? I didn't know that. I think **it looks and tastes like eggy fish**! Dad says it's an 'acquired taste'."

She said **"acquired taste"** using squiggly fingers to wrap around the words, like grown-ups do, and in a funny voice. I couldn't believe it, **Evie had made me laugh**. I'd spent so long being annoyed with her that I'd forgotten I liked her a lot when she first started school.

"I like fried dumplings and brown-stew chicken," I told her, relaxing a little.

"Yeah," Evie agreed. "I love chicken! Jerk chicken's my favourite."

"Yeah, that chicken's a real jerk," I said. We both

laughed out loud. I don't know why, it wasn't even funny.

Mrs Grace, who looks after the room known as our library, shushed us from her desk. We giggled quietly.

"I'm sorry about your grandad," said Evie, adjusting her hairband. "I didn't come to the nine nights with my dad because I didn't want to upset you again. I shouldn't have said that to you about him... I didn't know he was ill... Well, it was just wrong anyways — and your grandad was a very nice man. **I am really sorry, Sunshine. Truly sorry.** What happened in the playground, all the pushing and shoving...it was my fault—"

"It's okay," I interrupted. She was struggling, I could tell. And it was okay, I knew she meant her apology about Grandad.

"My mum had cancer too," she declared. Evie looked so relieved to say the words, like she had just put down a school bag full of encyclopaedias that she'd been carrying on a ten-kilometre walk.

"Oh! I'm so sorry." I *was* sorry. This was a shocker. I didn't know what to say.

Evie sat down and 'fessed up everything.

"She's in remission."

"What does that mean?"

"The cancer's gone away, but she has to keep getting checked to make sure she's all right."

"Well, I'm glad she's okay." I tried to smile reassuringly for her. I looked at Evie. She was wringing her hands as if she was squeezing out a dishcloth.

"I just wanted to make it better, to make her laugh, to make her eat, to make her be alive. I'm sure I must've got on her nerves. I tried so hard. I hate cancer… I hate it so much that when Mum was really ill, I dreamed about it every night — that it was a real person and then I would hit it the hardest I could, every single time, but it wouldn't go away. I was so tired from all the dreaming and then each day **I woke up and it was like living in a nightmare.** Does that sound stupid?" she asked.

Did that sound stupid? Not to me it didn't. I shook my head.

We were both silent for what felt like hours, but only a few seconds of stillness had passed by.

"Why didn't you tell me?" I asked.

"She had it for a long time and that's why we moved here, to be closer to Mum's family. We even had the dream holiday to Italy last summer because we were trying to enjoy every moment. But I was so worried that I didn't really like the trip that much. Everyone told me that I needed to be strong, to keep my chin up. So when I came to a new school, I didn't want anyone to feel sorry for me. And if I talked about it, I knew I would cry. So I tried to be a super happy me. **And I tried to be like you.**"

"Like *me*? You think I'm silly and boring. Silly Sunshine!" I said, almost shouting.

Mrs Grace shushed at us again from her chair. In the circumstances, I know it seems childish, but I had to get it off my chest. "And you said things that weren't so nice. I don't do that."

"You said I looked like a fish." It was Evie's turn to get things off her chest.

"I said you pouted like a fish."

"Like that's any better?"

I had obviously electrocuted Evie's nerves in the same way she had mine.

"What you said in the letter to your pen pal hurt my feelings…and some people at my old school used to make fun of my lips and my hair. I don't know why really, maybe it's because I looked different to everyone else. They'd say my lips were big and that my hair was really big and bushy when I loosed it out, and try and touch it all the time — that's why I always tie it up now," Evie said to me.

I shook my head in disbelief.

"So, it sounds silly, but the fish thing on top of everything else just upset me, I guess," she continued.

I guess sticks and stones may break bones, but **words can really hurt too**. But I'd only thought about that in relation to myself — not about how my own actions had hurt Evie. I would never have expected her to be so sensitive, because she is so clever, so beautiful. I can't believe she got picked on at her old school. I thought everything was perfect for her.

"I'm sorry, Evie. I'm sorry I hurt your feelings too."

Evie bit her lip. "I didn't tell you the complete truth when I gave you that card, Sunshine."

"O-kaay," I said, wondering what on earth she'd say next.

"I did know I was being mean to you," continued Evie. "I didn't do it on purpose at first, that's true. But then I could tell you didn't really like me…and then saying those things made me feel better… Then it made me feel miserable, and then I blamed you…and that made me worse. I just got so angry. But I don't think I was really angry with you.

"I didn't mean for things to go that far, I really didn't. Yes, you can be silly, but in a nice way. And you are not uninteresting, Sunshine. I said that because it's so *not* how you are. I didn't think someone like you would take it so seriously. **You have the coolest name in the world.** The coolest hair. You have a robot that lives in school reception. You even have the best birth story! And you're funny and you're smart. Maybe not as funny and as smart as me, but still…" She tailed off, half-smiling, but still half-looking like she could cry.

I smiled back warmly.

"Can we start again?" she asked.

I shrugged. "Sure."

A beam of sunlight suddenly burst through the window

and lit the floor between us. I looked out at the clearing sky beyond. Dissolving the drizzly grey, **the sun was politely asking the day to brighten**. I smiled as the beams stretched out like arms, tickling my face. I felt myself glowing inside. It was turning out to be a bright sunshiny day.

I don't know what will happen next. Maybe things will be the same again, maybe they won't. A little voice in my head tells me that any friendship between Evie and me won't be plain sailing.

I expect there will be ups and downs, and ins and outs. But that's the interesting thing about life. **Yes, I know Grandad**, I whispered to myself, **you were right. It's an adventure.**

Sunshine's Notes on Black History

Windrush

Imagine what it feels like to pack up all your things and move to a country far away from home! Well, on June 21st, 1948, a ship called the *Empire Windrush* arrived in London at Tilbury Docks. On board were hundreds of people from different countries in the Caribbean, such as Jamaica, Trinidad and Barbados. I hope no one on board was seasick because it was such a long way to come!

Between 1948 and 1971, around 500,000 people from the Caribbean made the journey to the United Kingdom. It must have been a very scary or maybe an exciting experience – perhaps even a little bit of both!

The "Windrush generation", as they became known, came to fill job vacancies like in the National Health Service and railways, and worked tirelessly to help Britain get back on its feet after the Second World War.

The Windrush generation has also helped to shape British culture; writers such as George Lamming and Sam Selvon wrote about their experiences coming to Britain. And calypso singer Aldwyn Roberts, under his stage name Lord Kitchener, sang the now-famous "London is the Place for Me" for reporters when the *Empire Windrush* arrived. It's a really bright and happy song. Maybe that's why they used it in the film *Paddington* because it makes you smile!

Bob Marley

changed the world with his music.

Bob Marley is one of my parents' favourite reggae artists and was one of the most famous musicians in the world.

Reggae music takes traditional Jamaican folk music called mento and mixes it with other popular music including American jazz and R&B, ska and rock steady.

Jamaica

The thing I love most about it is that it sounds very chilled, but a lot of Bob Marley's songs are about important things like injustice and freedom.

He formed a band called The Wailers, and introduced people worldwide to Jamaican music and culture with songs like "One Love", "Get Up, Stand Up" and "Redemption Song".

My favourite song is "Three Little Birds".

Mary Seacole

helped those in need.

Mary Seacole was a British–Jamaican nurse who made her mark on history.
In 1854 she travelled to England and volunteered to join the nurses working to care for soldiers wounded in the Crimean War. She was turned down for this job, but went to the Crimea by herself and set up her own hospital.

She called her hospital a "hotel", and did more than treat injuries. She gave her patients hot food and warm clothing so fewer soldiers would die from hunger and cold. She was even known to ride onto battlefields on horseback and tend to injured men while under fire.

Mary returned to Britain in 1856, but she had spent all her money on her hotel. Luckily, people had heard of her good deeds and donated money to help her, wanting to recognize her selflessness. Mary received medals for her bravery.

In 1857, Mary wrote her autobiography, and it became a bestseller. Go Mary!

**Read on for a sneak peek
of the next**

SUNSHINE SIMPSON
ADVENTURE

The phone was blaring. Dad answered the call. All our heads swung in his direction.

"Who on earth is calling us on the house phone?" muttered Mum.

At first, Dad couldn't hear who was speaking on the other end of the line. "It's a bit noisy, can you speak up, please?" Dad shouted.

But then Dad's face changed. His expression became contorted, his voice sounded crackly — a bit like the bad phone line. "Where? But how? No!...Yes!" Whoever it was on the other end of the line had really hit their stride, and Dad was barely getting a word in edgeways.

Curiosity got the better of the rest of us and we'd all gathered in the hallway behind Dad. He was silent as he finally put the phone down. His hands were trembling.

"What is it?" Mum asked, urgency in her voice.

"It's…it's your mother," said Dad, quietly.

"What's happened to Mum?" screamed Auntie Sharon. "Is she sick? Oh no, is she—!"

Dad waved his hands in front of him to stop Auntie Sharon from saying any more.

"No, no! She is very much alive and well."

Everyone seemed confused. What had happened to Grandma Pepper?

Dad looked straight at Auntie Sharon and Mum, who were hanging onto each other for dear life.

"For crying out loud, Tony, what is gwarning?" exclaimed Auntie Sharon.

"She's here. She's in England. Your mother's at Birmingham Airport!"

"Lord have mercy!" cried Granny Cynthie as Grampie Clive steadied her.

"What on earth is Pepper doing here?" We all swung round. It was Mrs Turner. Who let her in?

"I've changed my mind," said Auntie Sharon, "Someone get that bottle of wine."

As for Mum, I'd never seen that expression on her face before. She looked empty. Spent. Gone.

It was dawning on me that I was probably in the biggest trouble of my whole entire life. This chaos was all my fault. I shouldn't have sent the letters.

 To find out what happens next, don't miss

SUNSHINE SIMPSON
COOKS UP A STORM

A NOTE FROM ME TO YOU

Hello,

My name is G.M. Linton and I am very pleased to meet you.

In fact, I can't really believe I'm writing this note!

When I was ten years old, I was very shy and quick to be intimidated by most situations. I struggled with confidence, despite the love and care I received from my family. I definitely admire Sunshine for finding the courage to walk out onto a stage and perform in front of an audience. And I'm glad I found the confidence to eventually write this story.

I was born and brought up in the West Midlands. My parents, like Grandad Bobby, were from Jamaica, but migrated to England in the 1950s. My mum was a nurse, who worked for the NHS for three decades, and my dad was a carpenter who helped build many of the motorway networks and houses that we use and live in today.

I was born a couple of decades later in the 1970s (yes, I'm that old — but I was still young enough not to have to suffer the indignity of wearing flared trousers!). As I grew up, sometimes I found it hard to find my place. Was I more English or Jamaican? Did I have to choose between the two?

I was unsure about so many things, but the one thing I did know was that I most-definitely wanted to write books. I loved to read, and even though there weren't any stories I remember reading with characters who looked like me, I would still devour the pages of the books in front of me and make up my own stories and characters. But somehow, over the years, the dream of writing faded and was replaced by growing up and doing other things.

But then one day a few years ago, I remembered something. My parents used to sit in the front room of our family home and tell their grandchildren, and my siblings and me, stories about their lives "back home" in Jamaica and what it was like coming to live in England. After hearing the same stories so many times over, I (shamefully) didn't always pay the greatest attention. But then as I watched my parents grow older, I realized something very important — their stories of travelling on their own to a strange land, leaving their relatives and friends behind, and adapting to a new way of life, were actually very interesting indeed. I wanted to capture their stories in words, because I knew they wouldn't always be here to share their life journeys with us. So, I decided to open my ears and listen, and to remember what I had heard, but often ignored.

When I started to write this story, I had a few things in mind:

1) I wanted to write something about the special bond that is shared between children and their grandparents.

2) I wanted to remember what it felt like at the beginning of growing up.

3) And I also wanted to remember my parents and people like my parents, who are now collectively known as the Windrush generation. These special people were very important in the journey of rebuilding post-war Britain — and they have brought a richness to society that hasn't always been recognized in the positive ways that it should.

I have now lost both my parents. No, that's not true. I haven't lost them, because their memories, their sayings, their humour, and their kindnesses, live on in my heart and, hopefully, in the words and spirit of this book. Even though Sunshine's story is the story of a fictional family, my parents' input and guidance over many years has helped me to write it. I'm so proud of them for what they achieved in their lives and I want their voices to be heard.

By the end of this story, Sunshine finds her voice, even though she realizes there will be more twists and turns along the way, because that's life. It took a long while for me to figure out how to be me, and I'll let you into a secret — like Sunshine, I'm still working on it, because I've learnt that life is often about growth, development and change — making mistakes; learning from mistakes.

And it doesn't matter how big or small your dreams are or how long it takes for you to achieve them, just keep at it. If I hadn't decided to try my best and write this book, I wouldn't be writing this note to you.

As Grandad Bobby says, "See your life as an adventure. It's yours to live, so live it the best way you can. Do your thing and don't hesitate. Go for it! And if you fall down, get up and go again... Life is always an adventure. Never forget that."

And in answer to my question: am I more English or Jamaican? The answer is, I am both. I am English with a rich Jamaican heritage. I am Black British. I am me.

Be you.

ACKNOWLEDGEMENTS

Perhaps I've come to my favourite part of telling this story — thanking all the people who have helped me along the way.

Firstly, thanks to you, dear reader, for taking the time to read this story in the first place. (Unless you've started with the acknowledgements, to which I'll say, after you're done, please go back to the beginning!)

Thanks also to my agent Claire Wilson, who is, quite frankly, with the notable exception of Muhammad Ali, the greatest! Claire championed this story from the off — and has been a brilliant guide ever since. You are a genius or magic. Probably both. Thanks also to Safae El-Ouahabi and everyone who has supported me at RCW.

To my editors, Stephanie King and Rebecca Hill, who are so kind, so skilled, and so incredibly patient. You trusted me to tell the story I needed to tell, and believed in its simplicity from the start. Thanks also to all of the amazing team at Usborne, including Sarah Stewart, Alice Moloney, Fritha Lindqvist, Katarina Jovanovic, Hannah Reardon-Steward, Jessica Feichtlbauer, Beth Gooding, Deirdre Power and Christian Herisson. Will Steele and Katharine Millichope — for her cover design — get an extra special mention for putting up with me. Thanks to Fuuji Takashi, illustrator extraordinaire, who has really captured the essence of Sunshine and her friends. And to Emily Bornoff, who has done an amazing job on the additional inside illustrations. Thanks also to Alexandra Sheppard and Georgina Kamsika, for their extremely helpful insights as sensitivity readers, and to Gareth Collinson, for his proofreading prowess.

A special shout out to the WriteMentor programme. The feedback I received from the anonymous judges (children and adults) in your annual competition gave me the belief that I was on to something with this story. Stuart White, WriteMentor's founder, won't remember, because he helps so many people, but he gave me some first-class advice. And author Tasha Harrison very kindly gave me feedback on early chapters. If you haven't checked out WriteMentor, please do; it's a great resource for children's writers.

To my fellow Usbornites, PJ Canning, Cat Gray, Clare Povey and Dave Owen, this experience has been made even richer for meeting you. Thanks also to Serena Patel and her husband for their advice. There are so many lovely people in the children's writing community.

I also want to give a special mention to those teachers who nurtured a shy, young kid. Mr Davis, Mrs Callaghan, Mrs Langley, Mr Gill, and Mrs Basudev — thanks for everything. And to Pete Bennett — what an extraordinary teacher you are. I'll never forget your enthusiasm and how much you believed in me.

To my friends (sorry to miss anyone out — that's the trouble with listing names): Amanda, Angela, Ben, Brenda, Caroline, Donna, Helena, Karen (the best writer I know), Maureen, Mike, Jessica, and Stephen (and Otto!), who are always so very supportive. To Steve who, unbeknown to him, really gave me the confidence to believe I could write again. And to Maria, who is never forgotten. Thanks also to Russell, for your belief and encouragement, and for always being you.

Ooh, I'm sure I've forgotten someone...

Jokes! Not really! My siblings, Ivor, Hilary, Alison and Rose, and my nephews and nieces, are inspiring and wonderful. A special thank you to Alison for your help. You deserve a badge. No, a gold medal. And to Hilary for being a brilliant cheerleader! To my children, Mimi, Lissy and Mikey — my (very!) honest advisors — love you, and thank you.

By no means least, I want to thank my beloved parents. I owe them the greatest debt — and always will.

Finally, I give thanks to the Most High. My faith may ebb and flow like the waves of the sea, but you still keep me afloat, whether I'm sinking or swimming.

Don't miss Sunshine's next adventure!

SUNSHINE SIMPSON
COOKS UP A STORM